Whispers of Our Knowings

Whispers of Our Knowings

Laughing Womyn Ashonosheni

Writers Club Press
San Jose New York Lincoln Shanghai

Whispers of Our Knowings

Writers Club Press
an imprint of iUniverse.com, Inc.

For information address:
iUniverse.com, Inc.
5220 S 16th, Ste. 200
Lincoln, NE 68512
www.iuniverse.com

ISBN: 0-595-15227-9

Printed in the United States of America

This book is dedicated to spirit walkers and spiritual seekers everywhere.

CONTENTS

ACKNOWLEDGEMENTS

Thank you to all who have walked beside me in spirit. Special thanks to Rosie for your many years of patience and sometimes impatience with my learning. To Jody for bringing me new lessons in combining freedom with integrity. And to Suzanne for helping me hold this vision to completion. May all of your paths be blessed.

INTRODUCTION

The stories in this book are modern mythology and invocations to our souls. Goddesses and gods from a wide variety of cultures are mixed together to help us gain a clearer vision of some of the places we've been and others to which we can go as beings of light. The mixing of cultures, lifestyles and species is intentional. The mixing of "mortals" and "deities" is also intentional. We are one and this is an invitation to look to ourselves as the creators and overseers of our lives. We can indeed live with the integrity, wisdom, compassion and joy that we've previously assigned to our gods and goddesses.

I honor that which is most passionate, delighted and sacred in each of you.
Laughing Womyn Ashonosheni

Beginnings

CALL TO WILD WOMEN

The contrary-wise leaping of questing women brings us, the positively revolting willful women, to the doorstep of curious Sarasvati.

Sister, mother, daughter, seeker, leaving no stone unturned, no truth unturned. Contrary women who must question all, invent what cannot be questioned, turn all upside down and downside up until the top and bottom, inside and out can no longer be seen as separate, but as the same and yet different still.

We, the positively revolting willful women, dance widdershins at the doorstep of Sarasvati, moving always contrary to what is believed, to what is known. Finding in our contrary dance what is not known of the known, what is denied and hidden of the known.

Our contrary-wise leaping makes us questing women, seeking women, contrary, willful women. Hexing hags who will our way out of fool-dom. Hexing hags who's leaping dance in contrary ways, in woman ways, brings us always to Sarasvati's doorstep, our doorstep, our home step. One step out of, one step into, our homes, our hearts, and accepted truth falls before the laughter and questing of positively revolting willful women be-laughing our way through the wilderness of women's wildness, through the curiosity of Sarasvati, into the answers we need, the answers we know, the daughter-right of our births.

Questing women leap into ourselves, name ourselves, announce ourselves as the oracles we are, breaking the mirror of deceit that keeps women tamed, framed, within the mirror, the cage.

Hexing hags leap widdershins, whirling up positive revolts into women's ways of wildness.

Willful women turn the stones; question the questions as well as the answers.

Positively revolting willful women, hoards of hexing hags spin beyond the compass and reclaim your sense of direction!

REMEMBER

Return, return, sisters, with me to the time of our origin. Remember First Woman, great great great great grandmother, she who walked Earth when the land was still damp from birth, the mountain peaks jagged and covered with fuzzy, newborn, grass hair. Remember First Woman, she whose body was made from this Earth, molded and shaped to carry and birth the coming generations of children, of ideas, of human ways of being. First Woman looked upon Earth, upon her mama's body, and knew she was loved.

See me, sisters, daughters, sacred, holy women. Walk with me through this newborn grass. Inhale the fragrance of the flowers, the trees, the waters, the other Earth Walkers. Touch the silky soft hairs of First Bear, First Bird, and Cat. Slide your fingers across the warm smooth body of First Snake and the cool smooth body of First Fish. Allow Lily to curl around your fingers, Butterfly to wander through your hair. Feel Mother's essence, Mother's body, in all of your siblings.

We danced, sisters. We danced for eons under the light of our mother's mother, Grandmother Moon. In the velvet dark of star filled, full moon nights we began our dancing with the drums calling us. Mother's heart-beat called to us and we came together and we danced her heartbeat. Our bare feet caressed her skin late into the night, massaging her belly as she birthed ever more of her wonderful, magikal children.

And we slept, sacred, holy women. We slept deep and peaceful, embraced by our loving circle of kinfolk, all safe on the belly of Mama, all warm and breathing easy. We loved our dream time, the time when our souls flew to other realms to visit our cousins, the children of Mother's relations throughout the universe.

By day, as Mama's lover caressed her body with heat and light, we wandered among the grasslands and the tall standing people, our rooted relatives. We wandered and visited one another, sharing food and laughter, breaths of time together. We shared our lives, our warmth, our joy with all we encountered, greeting one another with open arms and the words, "I am you. You are me."

Remember sisters, when we gave birth to words, and writing, and counting. Remember when we learned to decorate ourselves and our homes, when we began wearing our sacred stone relatives so we and they could experience more adventures. Remember the first music that reached our ears, a gift from the winged people.

We sang sacred, holy women. With clear, open throats and sounds full and round, like our bellies, like us. We sang as we danced under Grandmother Moon. We sang our homes, our clothing, our nourishment into being. We sang and danced with our lovers, creating winding, wandering stories of our lives. We sang and danced with our children, teaching them laughter and wholeness.

Remember our laughter, sisters. Our belly deep, shaking, rolling, laughter. Remember that laughter rising forth from our toes, born out of our delight in ourselves and each other. Remember it tickling our hearts and filling our days. We laughed long and full for life is exquisite.

Remember our healing ways, our artwork, our ways of expressing ourselves, surrounding ourselves in beauty. Remember our strong muscles and bones, our minds that fly with our souls. Remember, sacred, holy women, wise ones whose bodies still carry the blood, the cells, the essence of First Woman. Remember; all that we have been, we are. All that we dream, we are. All that each of us is, we are.

Remember First Woman, great great great great grandmother, she whose womb brought forth all other humans. She who walked Earth when the land was still damp from birth... remember...

CALL TO WILD MEN

Come forth! Dance in the magnificent light of beauty. Reach deep inside yourself to the roots of all that makes you man. Listen brothers, sacred, holy, men. Listen to the roar of thunder that is the sound of new lands being formed, of new lives being born. Listen deep and call forth the roar of creation from within yourself.

Step into what we know, step into what we do not know, and see the good in all that is known and yet to be known. Dance; sacred, holy, men, dance until dust rises around our stomping feet and envelopes our bodies, clouding our vision so we cannot pretend to know that which stands before us. Dance to the unknown within and without. Dance life into the questions that have not been asked. Dance until the clouds of dust are blown free by the wildness of our breath, until the noon sun shines hot upon us and draws our cleansing sweat from deep within. Dance; sacred, holy, men, stomp your feet to match the heartbeat of our great Earth, to match the rhythms of birth and death. Dance life into all within and around you. Laugh deep in your belly and bring forth tears of joy, bring forth roars of mirth as you shake the foundations of the known so deeply the unknown comes rushing forth to be embraced, to be lived, to be us.

Create that which you desire. Leave behind that which restricts and dance into that which frees. Loosen your arms, your legs, your body from all that says, "I can't" and step fully into, "I can and I am".

Come forth! Dance in the magnificent light of beauty!

RETURN

Return with me now brothers, men of ancient times, modern times, and all the places in between. Return, sacred ones, to the memories of First Man, he who walked on Earth's belly as a young boy, curling his toes into soft mud and laughing at the texture. Return with me now to this time before we counted time, this time when all possibility stood ahead and all memories were intact, when First Man walked in the wilderness of all that is.

Feel the awe brothers, as we look out upon the jagged mountains, the dry desserts and wild oceans. Feel the awe, sacred, holy, men, as lightening flashes across the sky, quickening all in his path with the magnitude of his energy. Take in his gifts, smell lightning's smell and remember what it is to create a new world, a new reality, a new sphere in which life can become.

Dance the good dance brothers. Join hands and dance Earth's heartbeat and Sky's song. Remember song first coming to our ears from our bird cousins. Remember fire teaching us to cook food and warm our homes. Remember brothers; the days and days of walking we did on this vast Earth, encountering only friends along the way. Remember our hearts beating in unison, all of Earth's children knowing the joy of right relationship. Remember sacred, holy, men, the dance of Moon, Sun and Stars, the connection of all to the great center of all that is. Remember that we are one, Earth, us; Sky, us; Moon, us; winged ones, four leggeds, and swimmers, us.

Look out from the vastness of our beautiful home to the greater vastness of the Milky Way and know that we are joined; we are brothers, each related to each star in that vast family of stars. We are brothers, each related to each star in this vast family of stars.

Look in brother, in to the vastness of our own souls. Remember who you are, who you've always been. Look in brothers, sacred, holy, men, and bring your mind and your heart into a common walk. Join all parts of yourself with all parts of all that is and resonate with the oneness of all beings that is our wholeness brought to life. Feel your wholeness, feel your place within wholeness and know that you are.

Reach within brothers, sacred, holy, men. Reach within and find that place where your heart resides. Touch the fullness of your heart and know that it is good. Remember when we knew brothers. Remember when we knew our beauty and lived through that wisdom. Remember the soft touches of our children, our lovers, ourselves as we lived the beauty within. Remember the beauty of our minds as we began to create, as we learned to make our lives and those of our loved ones easier. Remember brothers, sacred, holy, men, our gift, our legacy, is the beauty we create.

Remember and return with me now brothers, men of ancient times, modern times, and all the places in between. Return sacred ones to the time before we counted time, the time of First Man and all of his dreams and memories. Let's walk together on Earth's belly curling toes in soft mud and laughing from the very core of our beings as we re-member ourselves.

EARTH

Walk across Earth's gentle belly and know the great depth of soil and stone, the manifestations of Earth's essence. Look upon these majestic mountains and know the depth of passion that has pushed these masses of soil and stone up to meet Sky, Earth's delighted lover. Push your naked toes into soft mud and remember that you too are of this soil.

Lay belly to belly with Earth, as you would with any favored lover, and breath in the rich scent, listen to Earth's many voices, take in Earth's touch. Feel the heartbeat of your home, your essence, your self and know that you are one with the one who supports your feet and provides food for your belly.

Run your hands through Earth's grassy hair and across the flowers that celebrate this rich body and understand the delicious fullness of life. Give thanks, Earth Walker, for your magnificent companion.

AIR

Air swirls and plays, tossing leaves and sweeping through branches with uninhibited delight. Air blows fresh and cool, skimming across water on toes as light as the down of a bird's underwings.

Air blows harsh and cold with winter's frost, chilling bones and homes, sending all into shelter. Air blows fierce and wild, whipping up hurricanes, tornadoes and fearsome howls. Air sings through dark nights and wild storms, pushing fears to the surface and blowing away their debris.

Air fills our lungs and feeds our blood, cleansing our bodies. Air feeds our brains, allowing thoughts to move quickly and clearly. Air is creativity in motion, nothing solid, always moving, always exploring a new perspective.

Breathe your being into Air. Breathe your essence into Air. Become that which surrounds you at all times. Live the light touch and irresistible presence of this one who knows no bounds. Fill yourself with the uninhibited delight of Air's joyful play.

FIRE

Fire licks up around my ankles, threatening to consume, threatening to transform all that I am and know into that which I am not and do not know. Flames with red orange tips, blue at base from the heat in their heart, climb up my body, swiftly raising my passion to a boiling point.

I cannot stand in fire. I am standing in fire. I call to the South, the one whose heart kindles all fires, whose dry hot breath prepares fuel so the fire may eat and grow stronger. I call to the South, the one who is passion, who is all that sparks life. I call that I may learn fire, that I may eat and become fire, that I may ride through life on a passionate flame and know everyday that I am here as part of the fire; to transform, to change, to make way for that which is not yet known.

Fire licks up around my ankles heating my skin like the tongues of many lovers, coaxing life to the surface of my skin, encouraging me to look deep and see that which ignites the flame. I look. I sit by the edge of the fire and stare into the flames. I feel my disconnection from the flames, my separation, and so I move closer and my eyes draw me to the white hot coals, red edges burning and disappearing, shaping and reshaping that which is real with each breath they consume.

Deep within I feel the flame ignite to a distant chant; shaping and reshaping that which is real. The fire, shaping and reshaping that which is real. This is my essence, my heart. This is what will bring me to you. Shaping and reshaping that which is real.

Fire licks up around my ankles, no longer threatening to consume, but rather inviting to ignite, to become that which I am not, yet.

WATER

Water rushes in, from streams and brooks, from rivers, lakes and oceans, from raindrops; sky water. Gurgling and laughing, humming a song along the backs of rocks and tree trunks, water speaks to us. Water rises within us in salty sweat as we use our muscles on hot summer days, and rushes in to cool our bodies, to quench our thirst, to bathe us in calm at the end of a long day.

Water comes to us accompanied by the Thunder Nation. Tapping on our windows as the Thunderers call out their greetings, Water beckons us to play. When we join in their playful dance, Water runs down our faces, tickling our skin everywhere. Water eases our work by raining on the flowers and vegetables and eases our breathing by dampening the dust.

Water rushes in, exuberant in springtime floods, covering the land and rearranging things. Water carves new gullies and valleys through rock, teaching the power of persistence. Water demonstrates the beauty of change, dancing lightly on the wind in her winter coat of snow.

Water moves through and into and around us always. Water is one of the four great elemental spirits of this planet without which even our blood would cease to flow.

Water rushes in, from streams and brooks, from rivers, lakes and oceans, from raindrops; sky water. Listen closely as Water speaks wisdom to us. Receive Water's essence and give of yourself in the ever moving ebb and flow, give and receive, that we call life. What gifts does water give you? For what will you give thanks?

SPIRIT

Spirit moves through, within, without, knowing no limitations. Spirit moves through, conscious, aware, freeing and seeing, knowing all. Spirit whispers soft assurance in the heart of fear, encourages alertness in the face of danger. Spirit opens hearts drawn tight and minds frozen in time. Spirit eases between cracks in foundations of rigidity and surprises us with knowledge of other ways. Spirit appears and holds us gently when grief would have us turn away.

Spirit calls and calls again, speaking all languages at once, and none. Spirit glides in currents of air, swims in swirling water, sits in earth and dances in fire. Spirit is. Spirit lives within and without, coming from and going toward, meeting in wholeness where time and space, all that is and all that is not are one, are inseparable, are you, and I. Spirit is. I am.

CANDLEMAS

Cuchavira emerged from the dark of the year into the growing light. In his time of seclusion, he had committed himself to bringing forth new life in this coming year. His desire was to live fully and passionately in every moment and he knew to accomplish this he must be born into a new way of being. Cuchavira stepped into light, where all could see him and he spoke his vision.

He was challenged immediately by Ghede, the old one who keeps what was. "If you live fully and passionately, Cuchavira, you will no longer be who you are. You will cease to be Cuchavira and become one we do not know."

Cuchavira did not expect this response and he paused on his journey to consider Ghede's words. He paused to consider what it would be to no longer be known by those he loved. Cuchavira heard the call to sameness. He heard the call to that way of being that soothes others with its predictability. He had no desire to be foreign to his loved ones; he had no desire to be separate from his passion.

Cuchavira thought for some time and then he saw the true challenge Ghede had given him. He understood the first step into his new way of being.

"And you Ghede, are you so settled into what was that you cannot know what will be?" Cuchavira looked steadily at Ghede, the most respected of his elders. He looked steadily and lovingly into Ghede's eyes and challenged him to step into new life.

SPRING EQUINOX

Sun and moon dance together on this day, one stepping forward and the other back, then reversing their order as they sit in full equality, dividing time evenly between day and night. It is the turning point, the day when each embraces the other and acknowledges their sameness. The day before one yields to rest as the other grows in vibrancy.

Moon has held the fullness for many months, shining bright into hours sun could not reach, holding time in place while sun moved into rest and then began awakening to warm earth and quicken all upon her. Now sun has awakened and is stretching fully, eager to shine warm and bright on all that would grow into new life during this cycle.

Sun and moon sit together on this day, holding earth and all her beings in perfect balance, in full equality. They sit and dance this day in our highest vision of equality. Look, watch sun and moon and see their steps, see their dance. See how both, each, have their own way of being. See how both, each, respects the other's way.

BELTANE

Earth lay quietly in her early spring blanket of old leaves and left over hints of winter's snow. Here and there fresh green sprouts showed themselves, promising more vigorous growth to come.

Telepinu walked Earth's gentle hills searching for his friend Frey and finally found him, sunning himself on a large mossy rock. Frey breathed in the sweet scent of life beginning to emerge as he absorbed the warmth of sun's strengthening rays and welcomed his old friend to join him on the rock.

"The day has come," Telepinu said, stretching his body across the rock and leaving a trail of fresh green everywhere he touched the mossy covering.

"And so it has," Frey responded. "I began my walk in the east this time, touching fields and trees, birds and many four leggeds. They've all begun to stir." He opened his arms wide and young ones of many sorts tumbled to the soft ground and began their new lives.

"I walked through the west. The waters are now playing freely over rocks, washing riverbanks clean of winter's remains. The trees have begun to flower and bees are exploring for nectar." Telepinu spoke softly. "Shall we go together to the north and coax her into play?"

The two set off for the north's cool regions, laughing and gently touching the new borns as they teased early spring into late spring's warmth in this slow to awaken place. Satisfied that the north was aroused from her lingering slumber, they made their way south, calling all to follow them.

By dusk Telepinu and Frey had gathered many Earth dwellers on the southern hilltops. Flowers bloomed in abundance amidst the long grasses and freshly leaved trees. Winged ones, two leggeds, four leggeds and all their relations breathed in the fresh scent of new life. Night and day merged together in the age old dance of joining and the very hills came alive as all gave thanks for the richness of life.

SUMMER SOLSTICE

Sul, old grandmother, she who dances daily from east to west through our blue sky, she who warms our home and lights our days, Sul is wide awake this day.

This day her strength has reached it's peak and lively Sul rises early, waking the birds to sing their melodies before Grandmother Moon has begun to consider setting. Sul caresses the still young corn, beans, and fragrant herbs. She moves softly across treetops, touching leaves with her life giving essence. Sul wakes the dogs and cats, warming their fur and tickling their noses, urging them to wake the people and begin this longest of new days.

And the people rise to Sul's call. They leave their beds and step forth into the gift of Sul's fullness, knowing this is the day when all they've planted during the season of rain steps into the vigorous growth that yields a harvest of great abundance.

The people move through this day, doing as they always do, and all the while thinking of their young crops; the ones in the field that can bring food to hungry bellies, the ones in their hearts that can bring nurturance to their ways of being with one another, the ones in their minds that can bring new ways of walking with spirit on this abundant Earth mother.

As this longest day of the year draws toward a close, the people prepare themselves to celebrate this herald of the turning of the seasons, this time of high light that balances the time of high dark on the other side of the year. They gather joyfully around their summer fire, the spark of Sul's great energy that lives on Earth. Laughing and playing and dancing the people draw this year's new life into vigorous growth, knowing the harvest of their labors will follow soon.

And Sul, old grandmother, she who dances daily from east to west through our blue sky, reaches her resting place in the west and eases herself into a nap before beginning her dance again.

LAMMAS

Ceres stands on the hilltop, her companion Dionysus at her side. They survey the bountiful fields, vineyards and orchards below and each smiles in satisfaction. It is indeed time for first harvest.

Dionysus sounds his horn, sending the long clear notes across the land from hilltop to hilltop, pausing briefly in the valleys to awaken any who linger there in sleep. And the people begin to emerge. They come forth from houses and out from amongst the trees. They carry big empty baskets from their barns and sheds and dance their way into the fields, singing songs of celebration as they go.

The baskets are filled with vegetables and fruits, all that they can eat and a little more. As the fields are harvested of most of what's ripe, care is taken to leave untouched what has not ripened and to leave ripe foods at the edges of the fields so the forest dwellers and winged ones can set their own feasts for this day.

Baskets ladened with plenty, the people return to their homes and begin preparing food for winter storage and for the harvest feast. They gather in groups to wash, slice, and spread fruits and vegetables for drying. They make preserves and relishes, and snitch bites here and there.

As the day moves toward dusk, the choicest foods of the harvest are brought together and given to Ceres and Dionysus in thanks for their nurturance of the young crops. And the people prepare soups, pies, salads and many wonderful delicacies. The air is filled with laughter and tantalizing aromas as recipes are traded, bites tasted, and stories told of harvests past.

Dionysus entertains all around him with the story of the year so many grapes grew that the people couldn't dry them in time to prevent spoiling. The spoiled ones were cast aside in a pit and then the rain came, fermenting the grapes and sending purple juice spilling into the paths. It was one of the village dogs, thirsty from his play, who discovered the effects of those fermented grapes.

As the stories and laughter spiraled among the people, the sun dropped out of sight and night arrived. Feast tables were set and late into the night; the people joyfully celebrated one more abundant cycle of life.

Fall Equinox

As summer's full bloom passes into the clear blue skies and first cool nights of fall, our year is turning toward rest. Moon is edging toward greater fullness, taking a little more time for night, leaving a little less for day. And the day arrives when eggs will stand on end, when Earth is so perfectly balanced between light and dark that round, fluid filled containers of life will not tip to the pull of gravity. The day arrives when Earth's magnetic field supports perfect balance and harmony. This is a day of peace. This is a day of self-created action; a day when outside influences cease to have their usual effect and each of us is supported in living a new reality.

See the wonder of this magical time; round, fluid filled being who is pulled like the tides by gravity's desires. See the wonder of this day of rest, this day when nothing outside of you can affect your center. Feel this day and know what it is to be your own source of gravity. Take this wisdom with you into all of your other days and know one of the great mysteries; the source of your own gravity, that which keeps your feet on this plane, is you.

HALLOWMAS

At the midnight hour the clouds gathered, hugging the edges of the bright, full moon, the only light in an otherwise dark black sky.

The trees of the sacred grove lifted their leafless branches, dark silhouettes against the dark sky, praying the whispered prayers of those who live their lives rooted to one place.

The two leggeds, four leggeds, and the winged ones gathered in this sacred place grew still. The silence became thick, hanging close to all present like a heavy wool cloak on an icy night.

From the dark silence, a soft voice emerged, "I invite Am-mit, She who takes back that which has been born to her." Those present breathed their thoughts to the east.

Another voice appeared, "Hakea, ruler of the Land of the Dead, sister and friend to Pele, I call you to join our circle!" With great enthusiasm, passion was thrown to the south. And silence returned.

"I call to Citallinicue, the one who rides the Milky Way and lights the path of the dead, be with us now." Soft sighs carried the emotions of all in the grove to the west.

"Sedna, mother of the swimmers and four leggeds of the frozen north, She who welcomes our spirits to the depths, I invite you to our circle." Silently, the most ancient memories of the gathered ones drifted to the north, then reflected their energy to the center where stood the oldest, most wizened, and wrinkled of crones imaginable.

"I, friends, am Hekate, The Old Woman Who Never Dies, the voice of all those you have called. I am She who always and forever stands at the heart of the crossroads. On this night of the crossroads, when the mist between the worlds parts, I have come to you."

With a loud cackle, Hekate threw open her dark robe, fluttering it's edges high over the tree tops until it became one with the night sky. Bats and owls and other night flyers shook loose from it's folds and flew in circles around the grove before settling in with those already assembled. Cats, green eyes flashing in the moonlight, coyotes, wolves, and the whole chorus of night singers, crept outward from her feet and joined the circle.

When all had settled, Hekate gave three shrill whistles. Wind answered her call, blowing away the last clouds and the last wispy fingers of mist.

"Those gone before and those yet to come have wisdom for you who are; have memories for you who are; have knowledge for you who are. Listen, look, and know." Another loud cackle brought forth a panorama of sights and sounds in the sky, around the grove, and in the air.

"Travel into the hearts and bones of your ancestors. Know that they who have come before, and you who are; are they who have yet to come. Know how ancient your memories are; know how current is the wisdom of those memories. Know the mystery of this spiral dance of life that moves ever outward only to circle again into the center."

The grove breathed as one. The spirits, the trees, four leggeds, winged ones and the two leggeds, all breathed and moved as one, watching, hearing, feeling and knowing. The spirits danced and sang for those in bodies, imparting all the knowledge that could be absorbed. Those in bodies danced and sang for the spirits, trading knowledge for knowledge until all were satiated and silence began to return.

A few more ancestors danced across the grove, one more breath was shared and the air thinned with a cool breeze. A sharp cackle, springing forth as a woman's shadow flitted across the face of the moon, called the gathered ones back to ordinary reality.

WINTER SOLSTICE

The Sun Keepers of the north and the Night Keepers of the south embraced their long mid-December sleep, the land to the north of their dwelling lay blanketed with winter's chill. The Sun Keepers of the north awakened each day only long enough to sustain life until their sleep could return the passion of summer to their bodies. The land to the south lay in full bloom of summer; the Night Keepers of the south waking only long enough to remind Gaia's dwellers the night would return.

The Night Keepers of the north, circled outside the dwelling with the Sun Keepers of the south, waiting to hand over the nurturance of Gaia's energies to their sleeping friends. The waiting Keepers knew the sleeping ones would awaken joyfully if Gaia's dwellers remembered their names and called to them with song, laughter, feasting and celebration. Each Keeper chose a favorite aspect of Gaia and called forth the dwellers of that direction.

Rait awakened the beings of Africa and her islands, calling them to bring forth frankincense and myrrh to bless and purify the awakening ones and lift their spirits.

Amaterasu called forth the beings of the Far East to hang pine branches over the house doors, insuring continual joy to all within.

Knowee and Yhi sang to the beings of Australia and all her sister islands to cast their sacred circles with evergreen leaves, weaving an everlasting wreath of sacredness and equality around all of Gaia's dwellers.

Nahar and Shapash breathed on the beings of the near east, asking them to call the pentagram, symbol of life and health, into the sacred circle.

Tecciztecatl inspired the beings of the Americas to give branches of holly for the circle, the red berries providing the menstrual blood of new life to the incoming season.

Nox and Nyx invited the beings of southern Europe to carry bells to the sleeping ones and ask their souls to awaken. Zorya Vechernyaya gathered the beings of northern Europe and her islands and together they planted the evergreen tree of immortality within the sacred circle.

As the dwellers of Gaia gathered, some donned robes of red to honor the fire of the sun, some robes of green to honor the life energies. Others donned robes of black to honor the peaceful casting of the night.

Four large candles were lit at the outer edge of the circle to encourage the sleeping Sun Keepers to awaken and shine brightly. Four small candles were lit to encourage the sleeping Night Keepers to awaken and allow their stars to glow.

Each of Gaia's dwellers placed a small ornament representing some aspect of life on the tree of immortality. When all the ornaments were placed, melodies began softly rising, gently calling forth the sleeping Keepers to look upon the faces and lives of those who love them.

The first to emerge were the Night Keepers of the south as their names sounded repeatedly around the circle; Hekate, Athtor, Meztli, Ratri. Hekate, Athtor, Meztli, Ratri... They were welcomed into the circle by the Sun Keepers of the south, who gifted them with the baskets that hold Gaia's southern energies. A slowing of life began immediately within the southern dwellers of Gaia, a peacefulness settling over them as they prepared to enter the resting of their year.

The circled ones began singing the names of the Sun Keepers of the north Hsi-Ho, Igaehindvo, Surya, Sul, Wurusemu, Lucina. Hsi-Ho, Igaehindvo, Surya, Sul, Wurusemu, Lucina... Slowly the circle brightened as the Sun Keepers of the north stepped in and were greeted by the Night Keepers of the north who gifted them with the baskets that hold Gaia's northern energies. The northern dwellers of Gaia felt a quickening in their blood as their Sun Keepers took hold of the energies. The singing became louder, melodies faster, and all began dancing. Gifts were exchanged among Gaia's dwellers in honor of the exchange of energy baskets between the Night Keepers and the Sun Keepers.

The dwellers of Gaia spread a feast to share with the Sun Keepers and the Night Keepers and thanked them for nurturing their mother's energies with such perfect balance.

And so is celebrated the awakening of the night in the south and the sun in the north.

Wanderings

ANCESTOR

During the last life cycle of her people, Hekate accepted the job of tutoring the new humans. When all had died except herself, she took the form of a very old woman and opened her womb one last time to allow the new humans to walk through her into their homeland.

When the passage was complete, the new humans honored Hekate, their gatekeeper between the Earth home and the land before and after time, by preparing a soft bed for her to rest upon until she recovered from the labor of their passage. They surrounded her bed with bright colored flowers and sang and danced for her amusement.

Smiling with the excitement of the new ones, the old woman whose face and hands carried more lines of wisdom than the hairs of a whole body, spoke to those she had promised to teach.

"The dance of my people has reached completion in this beautiful home, we move on to new adventures, new learnings. This home does not wish to be abandoned so we leave it to you who had no home to accommodate your adventures. There were others here before us and still others before them. As each began this part of their dance, they were asked by the one's before to dance here with honor, add their wisdom to the wisdoms already here, and pass this place on to the next new ones when their dance is complete. I ask this of you now. Your gaiety and excitement will carry you in many directions. You will learn much of yourselves here. As with all dances, you will do some parts right immediately, others will take much practice and involve many mistakes. Do not leave this home until you have learned each step that is here to perfection and added one round of your own steps.

Others will always inhabit this home with you. They too are your teachers and friends. Observe them, honor them, learn from them, and leave them to follow their own paths in their own ways. You will know who these others are because they are all the ones you encounter here who are not like yourselves."

Hekate paused for breath, brushed a wisp of shining white hair from her forehead, and lifted the youngest of the new humans onto her lap.

"As I am forever old to you, this one will be forever young. She will always remind you to take the next step with the excitement of new discovery. I will always remind you to take it with the wisdom of those gone before you. Dancing between and around the two of us will be you, the ones who will weave this young one's excitement for new experiences with my wisdom from past experiences.

Once in each cycle of the sun, when the trees are flowering with their new leaves and blossoms and the ground flowers are springing forth with the vibrancy of new life, join with your home and all who live here to celebrate the day you first walked here, returning youthful enthusiasm to the wisdom of the ages. Honor the old with the bright colors and fragrances of the flowers. Honor the young with song and dance. In this way, each will know the beauty of the other and wisdom and enthusiasm will walk hand in hand.

KARU

Karu walked across endless flat expanses of South America, seeing on each side of the land mighty oceans. Sun rose early over the eastern ocean, casting brilliant light all the way across the flat land to the western shore, where each night he came to rest in the waters of the west. Karu was greatly pleased with this vast land and called out to all sorts of other earth walkers to come join him, come play and live in this wonderful land of sun and water. And they came, the two leggeds, four leggeds, winged ones; the standing people, the fresh water swimmers and those of many legs.

Karu wandered among his relatives as they chose their new homes and he heard many speaking of Sun's heat and the long days that allowed almost no time for cooling at night. The standing people grouped their homes together to create shade for those who could not live in Sun's full joy, and still the heat was mighty. Karu walked to the eastern shore and blew gently across the land, freshening Sun's heat with the watery smell of ocean.

The land cooled and his relations found comfort in their new home and Karu knew that he could not stand forever thus, gazing across this beautiful land from the east shore and blowing his breath constantly to the west. He called together a council of all his relatives and asked for ideas to bring Wind to this beautiful land of sun and water. The land and water dwellers pondered this request and the winged ones swooped and glided above them, dancing wind's currents.

"We know Wind," called Parrot. "Wind loves our brilliant colors. We shall each drop a feather to the land and surely Wind will follow."

Soon the land was covered with brilliant reds, blues, yellows, and greens and Wind did follow, dancing with delight through all the colors, moving ceaselessly across the land and through the homes of Karu's relatives. And now they sought shelter from Wind, even the standing people could not entice Wind to slow this dance.

The other earth walkers asked Karu to send Wind away and to stand again on the eastern shore and blow his gentle breath across the land. Reluctantly Karu walked to the eastern shore and sat looking to the west. He had invited the others to come to this land of wonderful sun and water, but he did not want to become their servant. He thought long and hard about this dilemma and finally Wind joined him on the shore.

"Hills and valleys slow my speed," Wind told Karu, "I cannot slow myself without their help."

All Karu could see before him were endless days of breathing across the flat land and he released on long, frustrated sigh. Colors began to shift then, the feathers moving into ridges as Karu's sigh pushed them together, making the beginnings of hills. Karu and Wind looked at one another and laughed. Wind danced into the ocean, leaping and playing thru the waves, leaving land completely while Karu walked from east to west, breathing all the feathers into huge piles that became hills and then mountains. And when he was finished, Sun rose on the eastern shore and cast shadows of coolness across the feather mountains. Standing people climbed the mountainsides to bask in Sun's full joy, calling earth to join them and anchor the feather mountains to her belly. Karu's relatives then knew cool nights and sun filled days and their laughter and singing called Wind back from the eastern ocean to dance gently through their homes.

Ocean Journey

Changing Woman stepped forth from the sea, her hair entwined with lengths of seaweed, still wet and dripping water over her shoulders. Exhaustion and a slight smile of triumph adorned her face as her weary arms and legs carried her to the sandy beach.

Friends who had watched many days to see her emerge from the water greeted her on the beach. They took her to her resting place and held quiet vigil until the exhaustion left her body. She then began her story and her friends settled in for a long listen.

"I swam the ocean for this change because there are no landmarks there unless one dives very deep. If one swims shallowly, just a little below the surface, there is nothing stationary, no anchor, only colors and creatures that move and are never where they were when last you looked.

To find a way into the journey that would allow me to find my way back home I had to dive deeper than I thought my breath could carry me. At that great depth I struggled for air. I feared I would drown and never return from this journey. I feared that I had already gone so deep that I wouldn't have time to reach the surface before my air ran out. And around the edges of my fear, I saw landmarks; an odd shaped rock, a pink coral reef, a long dead tree trunk. These were the markers of my home place.

I looked ahead of myself and saw a cave inviting my exploration. Fear came to my awareness again and I thought of returning to the surface, to the air my body already knew how to breathe. And I asked myself if this journey felt complete yet, or if it felt unnecessary. It felt necessary and incomplete so I asked Fear to swim with me, to be my companion and protector, and we entered the mouth of the cave.

After swimming awhile in the cave, we found we could no longer see the entrance or find which of the many tunnels led to it. We had no choice but to continue this journey toward whatever end there would be. Fear stared me squarely in the face and screamed her rage at me for being so thoughtless. She screamed that my carelessness had removed her choices, was forcing her to continue doing something she thought was impossible. I screamed that she had agreed to be my protector and she had failed.

Then we both realized we had begun breathing the water, that substance our minds said we couldn't take in if we wanted to live. As the meaning of this loomed in our minds, we clung to one another, trying to gain strength and reassurance in this unfamiliar place.

After awhile I decided to continue the journey. My body seemed to be fine even though Fear insisted that was impossible. I asked her to keep going with me. I told her I'd rather die trying to stay alive than die staring at the walls of a tunnel I'd already been in for too long. She crouched in a corner and refused to go, convinced that what lay ahead on the journey would only be worse.

I moved away from her and back to her many times before I could leave her. Finally I grew impatient with my indecision and bade her farewell, releasing her from the duty to protect me. Fear's howls of rage echoed after me for a long time, beckoning me to return to that which had become familiar during our painful passage from air breathers to water breathers. I swam on.

When I thought I had been swimming from forever toward forever, I suddenly found myself in a huge domed cavern that sparkled from thousands of drops of water trickling down it's walls. The cavern was part full of water, part full of air, and part full of me.

Surprised to find myself in a place filled with my deepest wish, plenty of sweet, familiar air to breathe, I coughed the heaviness of water out of my lungs, took many deep breaths of air and sat down to sort through the teachings of this journey.

As the air massaged my lungs I looked around the cavern, searching for teaching signs. My mind came to rest on Fear who now felt both familiar and strange to me. What had been our attachment? Had I done what she said, I would still be breathing water, my lungs aching from its weight.

Had I done what she said before that, I would never have known that I could breathe water.

A woman, looking a lot like Fear, appeared at my side. 'I am your teacher,' she said quietly, 'you took in what was unfamiliar to you. You passed through that which was unfamiliar. You swam where you believed you could not survive.' Motioning to a tunnel she gently caressed my cheek and said, 'The door to home is here.'

I stepped through the tunnel and saw a long dead tree trunk, a pink coral reef and an odd shaped rock, and I knew my journey was complete."

GOD

"God is one supreme being, bigger than any of us, outside of all of us. God is each of us, human, four legged, winged, swimmers, stones, trees and all else. Each of us is God and ours is the responsibility to act as such. God is nothing but an imaginary concept created by humans with weak minds. And so the discussion has gone, for more generations of humans than any of us can count. Round and round the debate goes, it's whirling, spiraling energy giving birth to great leaps of human conciousness, to fights among otherwise loving people. It's spurred great acts of love and terrifying acts of war. And has all of this answered the question? Has it even defined the question? What is it we seek in searching through eons for God? Is the search not for one of higher wisdom, more all seeing vision, more loving countenance than we ourselves exhibit? Do we not search for that which loves unconditionally, that which interacts justly, that which gives us comfort in an unpredictable life?" Brigid stood, calmly watching for any effects of her words on those gathered in council. The peoples of Earth had been warring with one another for generations, and of late, the disputes had grown to the place where peaceful interactions were no longer the norm.

Brigid looked at Qat, into the black brown eyes of this man from the southern islands whose life had always personified love. "What do the people of your homeland seek in their relationships with spirit?"

"To better understand the ways of this place. The ways of living in these bodies that will feed all and deplete none." Qat breathed deeply of the cedar scented air and felt with his heart for the heart of each one present. "Our lives, if lived in the manner of our breathing, take in what is needed from the abundance around us and give back from the abundance within us. My people value harmony."

Gokarmo, robed for warmth on this chill day, leaned sideways into Skadi's shoulder, pushing her slightly off balance. Skadi pushed back upright, leaning against Gokarmo to hold her place in the circle. Gokarmo smiled at Skadi and leaned back with more force, again shifting Skadi off balance. Skadi returned her smile with a sharp look, warning her against further pushing and again pushed herself upright.

"So here it begins." Gokarmo said, smiling again at Skadi. "I leaned and pushed Skadi out of her place, she tried to regain her place and I leaned harder. Confusion about my intentions rose in her mind and anger would have followed soon for I had invaded her peaceful place in this circle of all beings."

"But even the plants, in all their peaceful existence, crowd one another out and force greater and greater space for themselves." Kuan-Ti's voice rose from the other side of the circle. He too was searching for lasting peace, unwilling to accept anger filled conflict as a necessary part of human experience, but he was tired of this conversation's shifting message. "Leaving each other alone, not expanding and changing as we grow, not moving about into other's home places has never been part of our being. We move, we get bigger, our minds expand with new knowledge. Never bumping into another is not the answer."

"And what of the conflicts over the nature of God?" Brigid tried to bring the conversation back to its original course, certain that was the basis for large-scale human conflict.

"It's an excuse," Kuan-Ti stated. "We search for arguments, for points of disagreement on which to pin our most basic fears. When the lies we tell ourselves build the energy in our bodies up to an unbearable point, we argue and fight with one another like children who desperately need sleep." His disgust with this whole discussion was obvious and some in the circle took offense at Kuan-Ti's obvious disrespect for the process of discussion.

Undertones of agreement and disagreement with Kuan-Ti's statements began to spread through the circle and Brigid saw the people finally coming to life, finally beginning to participate rather than observe. She knew this energy was what was needed for the people to create a new way of being. They rode into their future on the energy of disagreeing with their past. They grew more by hindsight than by vision. Brigid saw this and also knew the key to peace was in changing the stimulus for growth from hindsight to full enjoyment of the present moment. And she knew also that this was what spurred the search for one of more wisdom. If each human, each being whose mind could see clearly the past, could imagine the future and could experience and act only in the present, was focused fully on the present, then who would be watching the future to insure the actions of the present didn't adversely affect it? Who would insure that, if crops weren't planted today, the weather would be right tomorrow for planting? Who would insure that while the innocent played, they would not set up struggles for their own future? Brigid saw all of this and held her silence, waiting to hear what others would say. Waiting to see if the chain of self-deceit was ready to break or if there was still a need in humans to believe their own wisdom was too small to meet their needs.

AWHIOWHIO

Cernunnos stood atop the bluff looking into the forever land of Awhiowhio, He Who Stirs the Winds into a Whirling Frenzy. His path led directly through this land where all is never what it seems, and what it seems changes by the moment. From the bluff, Cernunnos saw the edge of the ocean, the heart of great Earth Mother, his destination. He carried with him two day's water, a bit of food and the land knowledge his grandfather's had given him.

Cernunnos knew that in the land of whirlwinds, of ever changing, his mind would not serve him well, only his feet, feeling the pulse of Earth Mother, and his heart, ebbing and flowing with her tides, would guide him to the great ocean of his quest.

Breathing deeply, inhaling the last hint of predictability that he'd know for this journey, Cernunnos began his descent from the bluff of clear skies into Awhiowhio's home and the whirling winds of change. A voice rang down the hillside behind him, "Cernunnos, hold your vision clearly. Cernunnos do not merge with the wind." The voice faded, leaving only its echo as the first blast of icy, hot, wind wrapped himself around Cernunnos body, pulling him a few steps away from his path.

Cernunnos struggled to return to the path and was embraced by yet another wind, this one smelling of ice flows, whispering into his ear, "follow Cernunnos, follow the ice." A gust of warm air, heavily scented with the early bloom of berries, blew across his face and Cernunnos followed the sweet scent, knowing surely this must be his path.

And the voice of Awhiowhio continued in his ear, deep and commanding, then light and playful, fierce and then comforting. "This way son. This way is the path to the ocean of man's heart." Cernunnos followed boldly, courage leading him as he turned this way, then that, heeding the old man's voice.

After many turns, and with no ocean yet in sight, Cernunnos found a rock and sat down to rest his weary muscles and very confused mind. He called to his vision, forcing his mind to focus again, pushing away the whispering voices of Awhiowhio. And Cernunnos remembered the wisdom of his grandfathers, the words meant for his feet and his heart, not his head.

The old men had showed him with their bodies how it feels in the soles of the feet to walk with spirit, how the feet feel their own prints enveloping them and singing the beauty of right relationship, for nowhere do the footsteps of one disturb the path of another. The old men's bodies had gently flowed around and through one another in the dance of open hearts. His own heart had reached out to join theirs in the soft, yielding manner of one who walks in balance with all that is and all that is not. Cernunnos remembered in his feet and his heart and the voices of Awhiowhio returned to his ears.

"This way Cernunnos! Follow the ice, follow the pines, follow the fire! Cernunnos, follow the scent of good food—it will lead you home!" And he turned, and turned, following the voices again. Then he stood still, Cernunnos, man seeking his heart, stood still, feeling Earth yield to his foot steps, foot prints enveloping feet and singing beauty to him. Cernunnos cautiously set one foot at a time upon Earth's belly, waiting to feel the embrace, to hear the song, moving each foot to a new place if embrace and song did not come. Soon, he felt Earth embracing his foot and heard her singing beauty even before each new step touched her. And he began to run, skipping and dancing across her belly, spinning Awhiowhio in a whirling dance as he went.

Awhiowhio's voices began to change, they no longer asked him to twist and turn, changing course every few feet. The voices blended into one long, rumbling laugh that surely came from deep within Awhiowhio's belly. The whirling winds blew aside and Cernunnos found himself standing at the edge of the ocean with a magnificent old man whose wild white hair whirled about him in all directions. The old man laughed, his eyes sparkling like diamonds under a brilliant sun, and motioned to Cernunnos to look at the ocean. There danced Cernunnos' grandfathers, feet stepping surely on waves and earth, bodies gentle and flowing through and around one another, laughter filling the air, arms open to Cernunnos, inviting him to join the open heart circle of men.

I Am

"I can and I am. I can and I am," Raka whispered the mantra to herself again and again, taking it as deep into her being as she could.

She knew, now that early adulthood had slipped into almost her mid-years, it was time to grab on and live life for all it's worth. Her journey to here wasn't so easy, but it got her here and she couldn't complain about that.

What Raka couldn't understand was why. Why was she here and what was she to do with this life of potential and time and experience? She knew she was well loved, yet she struggled to feel herself truly loving. She knew many of her talents and skills, yet none held her attention for long.

Raka walked through the woods around her home on this, her day of deciding, her day of trying to become I can and I am rather than any of the other realities she'd tried on.

Her good friend Kozah found her in the late afternoon, sitting beneath a sycamore tree much older than either of them would ever know. Kozah too had led a life that was less than wonderful. He'd whirled through his early years in such chaos that he'd created great pain for himself and all around him who could not view him with detachment. Kozah's unease with his earlier ways of being brought him this day to the sycamore tree and to the place of desiring a life lived fully or not lived at all.

As Kozah sat next to Raka and listened to her whisper, "I can and I am," he began to whisper with her. Their whispers grew into full voiced chants, then songs, then melodies wrapping around one another as they spiraled up the trunk of the old sycamore and spread like wildfire through the canopy of branches.

Raka and Kozah sang until their throats would give forth no more sound and then sat silently as their songs rained down onto them from all around.

In the silence, each embraced the choices they'd made in their lives. Raka had chosen to restrict her being to ways that never touched others. Kozah had chosen to expand his being in ways that forced others to engage with him.

Raka saw the beauty of containing her own energy and saw ways to live that beauty and be fully engaged in life.

Kozah saw the beauty of engaging intensely with others and saw ways to live that beauty and be fully engaged with himself.

And they sat in silence while the moon rose, then descended, and the sun rose to the fullness of noon. They sat and allowed the new wisdom to settle deeply within their bodies. Life began calling and as the whispers grew into full voiced chants, calling these two seekers into action, Raka and Kozah gave thanks to the old sycamore tree, embraced with full hearts and each returned home as I Am.

Blood Dream

Lucina sits under the circle of night sky; Old Snake Grandma curled around sky's edges with her tail held tight in her mouth. Lucina's womb blood flows freely into the earth below her as she contemplates what it means to her to be woman in this time.

Images of her mother, aunts, and grandmas, as far back in time as her mind can reach, dance inside her head. She searches her memory for the last woman of her lineage who sat thusly and allowed her blood to nourish Earth in this moontime ritual that is as old as time itself. It wasn't her mother, or either of her mother's sisters; they bled into pads and tampons and disposed of them as neatly and unceremoniously as possible. Nor was it her most recent grandmas, they too came from the culture of hiding woman's blood, of dealing with this as an inconvenience that must not be seen.

She sat a long time, well past the time of known names and faces, before she finally heard a distant voice, "Lucina, daughter of my daughters, I blessed the Great Mother too." Then another voice called, and another. Soon there was such a clamor of voices that Lucina knew she had reached her grandmothers that lived before the times of woman's shaming and bondage.

Anxious to reclaim the old ways, Lucina called out to her grandmas, asking them how they bled and what they did while they bled.

"I sat on a nest of moss," one answered, "and spoke to my grandmas as you speak to me."

"I sat in a swing over a rushing stream and mingled my blood with Earth Mother's" answered another old voice. "My friends and I laughed and played in our suspended chairs so there would always be joy among our people."

And the litany went on, voice after voice bringing the secrets of this most basic of women's rituals forward to a generation separated by so many years that there was no other way to teach or learn. Lucina listened until she could hear no more, and then a little longer.

She began to cry; grieving all that was lost to her people of the old one's ways. She grieved the dignity and honor that once belonged to women and had gotten lost or been stolen through the ebbs and flows of time. And while she grieved, she bled, giving back to Earth that which she no longer needed to hold. Finally the tears stopped, and the flow of blood slowed, and the scream that howled across one thousand years began to quiet.

And Lucina sat in this new born silence and looked at her mother and aunts and most recent grandmas. She looked at their lives and saw a little glimmer of the old ways still peeking through. She remembered her mother's tender caring the morning Lucina first bled, and the pretty gold ring with the red glass stone in it Mom gave her later that day. She remembered her grandmother's insistence that she use the pink bathroom at her house because that was for "us girls". It was the only room in the house that had the palest hint of blood red on its walls. She began to see how Grandmother had claimed her own woman only space with that custom. Boys and men could go into any other room in the house freely, but they needed special permission to enter Grandmother's pink bathroom. Girls and women could go there anytime.

She remembered her other grandma's insistence that she have time with her daughters and granddaughters without the men and boys "being underfoot". She'd send them off fishing or playing golf while the women and girls spent the day together.

As she remembered, Lucina began to see her women a little differently. Where there had been only images of women focused on men and designing their lives to support and accommodate men's wishes, shadows began to appear. She could see the old grandmas standing by the sides of her women and whispering into their ears, "The daughters matter. We are, you are, they are, the gates of life for all spirits who would live as humans. None can become human but through woman. All the daughters, whether they bear children or not, are the grandmas of the future." And her mother and aunts and most recent grandmas nodded and found ways to pass the message on, "The daughters matter, it is we women who decide if and when another generation will be born."

Lucina saw how the women of her family had laid the foundations for her. She saw that the circumstances of their lives might never allow them to celebrate women the way she did. She saw that the women for whom she was laying foundations would celebrate in ways she would never reach. Lucina saw the wheel turning; old women knowing the past more than dreaming the future, middle aged women working hard to reconcile the past with their dreams for the future, young women dreaming the future with little concern for the past.

Lucina, sitting under the circle of night sky, noticed Old Snake Grandma curled around sky's edges with her tail held tight in her mouth. She noticed the circle with no beginning and never ending and she knew that for her, to be woman in this time means to embrace the wisdom of the old grandmas, to learn from and honor the lives of her most recent grandmas, her aunts, and her mother, and to encourage the dreams of all women's daughters.

HOTEI

In the land of the rising sun, the place where each new day begins with a burst of orange against the pale gray of departing night, Hotei sat in a meadow under a red leafed maple tree, laughing at the new dawn.

His face was lined with many years of smiles and his eyes danced and twinkled, catching the sun's new light and bouncing it into the world around him. Hotei knows mirth all the way to his toes, which wiggled and burrowed into the thick, green grass he sat upon.

On this particular day, Hotei laughed under the red leafed maple tree until mid-morning and then set out for the city that lay just over the next hill. This city was crowded with many people who worked hard to enjoy their lives. Some rose before sunrise, others stayed up late into the night, tilling fields, baking bread, sorting through information, and doing all the other things people do to fill their time. Sometimes, laughter would burst into the city as moments of joy were shared, then all would quiet and the normal routine would resume. The days and nights sped by almost unnoticed in this busy city.

Hotei entered the city in the fullness of this particular day and all about him he heard vendors calling out to customers, machinery humming away at its various tasks and the serious voices of many people deeply involved in their business. Now Hotei had business too, and he engaged in it deeply everyday, but it was hardly ever with any seriousness and he looked about himself, a bit perplexed at the people of the city and their serious ways. He saw the old ones among them with lines in their faces that ran all upside down from frowning and creasing their brows in deep thought. He saw the young ones among them rubbing their heads and necks to ease tension-stiffened muscles.

Hotei heard short bursts of laughter and saw smiles that lived on people's mouths, not in their eyes and certainly not all the way to their toes and he might have walked away from the city right then had not the funny shaped tree stump caught his eyes. There it sat, in the middle of all those serious busy people, all lopsided and a bit rotted in the middle, with one sprig of red maple leaves sticking out of its side at a very strange angle. The tree stump just sat there, tickling every leg that came near it with those shiny red leaves. And Hotei knew he'd found a kindred soul.

He walked right up to the tree stump and sat his grand self on the rotted middle and began laughing. The people walked further away from the tickling tree stump, looking warily at the man with the dancing eyes who laughed at nothing that could be perceived. And Hotei laughed all the harder. He laughed for the leaves that tickled his arm, he laughed for the sun far above and the breeze on his face. He laughed for the awkward and confused looks of the people walking by. He laughed for the sound of his own laughter.

The sun began to set and still Hotei laughed and laughed and the people finally saw him as so strange and absurd that they too laughed. They laughed at the odd man on the rotting tree stump and shook their heads in disbelief as he laughed back. By nightfall the whole city rang with laughter as the story of Hotei on the rotted stump spread. And while the people laughed, Hotei left the city and returned to the meadow to burrow his toes into the thick, green grass beneath the red leafed maple tree and laugh into the night sky, satisfied that his day's business had been accomplished.

TO LIVE

Chasca sits in the whirlwind that is often her world these days. She looks to her right and sees spirals of potential, some sparkling, bright; some barely visible. She looks to her left and sees spirals of emotion, some surging with joy filled passion, some surging with pain filled passion. She looks behind her at the pattern of her life thus far, weaving and twisting, twining itself around her choices. Her choices, these words echo in her mind and heart as she tries to find peace with the current circumstances of her life. Chasca looks ahead and sees a vast open space, a void, waiting to be filled by her with her next choices and their results.

She sits on a slab of reluctance as hard as rock, unsure of her ability to make wise choices, unsure of what results she desires for her future. Her old wisdom tells Chasca that her most present choice is to determine whether she will sit still longer and wait for some clarity or whether she will choose to move because the time for stillness has passed.

This once and sometimes vibrant woman, who now usually holds her energy wrapped tight around herself like a cloak protecting her from a storm, contemplates her fears. Once she knew her power to manifest wisely and at will that which she desired. Once she knew her ability to glide gracefully through and with the results of her will made real. Now, she is no longer sure of either. Recently her choices have led her into dark chasms in her soul, some she's seen and turned away from before, some she's never seen or felt in other times.

Chasca listens as her friends assure her that all within her is there to know fully and this journey is a good one. She receives these words in her ears and they stop somewhere in her head and will not enter her heart which recoils from them in horror. She watches this reaction in herself and wonders where her strength has gone, where her vision has gone. She wonders why she pulls away from this growth rather than embracing it joyfully as was her way in the not so far away past. Many around her tell Chasca they wish they could embark on such an exciting adventure, such an expansive, open ended adventure as the one she now walks. And her heart screams from within, "this is not expansion but the destruction of all that I've been!"

In those words, she hears the whisper of the old one's voices, "all that dies shall be reborn, death must precede new life as surely as life must precede death." And Chasca cries tears to cleanse her of confusion, and the tears feel never ending as they wash across her exhausted heart. She looks deep within at all the possibilities before her and she contemplates death and asks what her growth would be with this possibility.

Hekate, the old one who cradles death in her womb and gives birth to new life, lays her hand gently on Chasca's heart and looks deep into her soul with eyes that reveal all wisdom. As Chasca is drawn into Hekate's eyes, she sees relief. She sees an end to her long and often pain filled journey through the land of her heart. She sees that her true journey is to explore her heart, through all its ways of being. Chasca sees a place in her heart that she has never seen before, and in that place sit happiness and laughter untouched by pain and fear. She's believed this place to exist only in fantasy for herself and most others whose paths have included so many sharp stones.

Chasca searches for the path to this place, wondering if death will take her there by providing her a fresh start without the burdens her heart carries from this time. "Perhaps yes, " whispers Hekate, "perhaps no. That's not the question."

Puzzled by this response, Chasca searches for the question Hekate alluded to. Looking to her right, where spin the spirals of all potential, she notices one spiral that is beginning to grow more defined and she reaches out to let it settle into her hand. As she gazes into the vibrant green of the spiral, her hand touches her heart and calls her into the wisdom that is present only when mind and heart are joined. "The true question that cries for answering is this; did you come to this life to experience spirit without flesh or spirit within flesh?"

Chasca looks up from the question into Hekate's old eyes, soft with the wisdom of much experience. "If you came to this place, you came to experience spirit within flesh," the eyes tell her, "find your fresh start in the path upon which you walk." Hekate fades from her view and leaves Chasca standing alone, feeling the enormity of the changes she has created in her life and not feeling the strength to carry herself to a new place of balance. Her tears flow freely again, death has appeared as an option, one of many that have come and gone as she tries to see clearly through the whirlwind. How many more options will she try to grasp before she finds a true one? How far to go before she can rest?

And so, Chasca takes one weary step toward the edge of the whirlwind, knowing that where she stands is where she must begin and trying hard to believe that where she desires to go is where she will be.

LEGACY

Man, step forth; come to the place of meeting. Step into the fullness of spirit and live from you heart, from you belly, from your inside out. Step forth and know that your place is in the center with all that is.

Bring forth the golden bough of your wisdom and share it with all. Bring it forth as an offering of peace and unity, as a gift, and let it go, to be used by the receivers in the ways they know.

Claim your true value in the wheel of life. Let your false value slip away and with it the urge to war and destroy.

Who are you man? On which foot do you stand in a world of peace and life giving? On which foot do you choose to stand? Do you know how to stand? Can you bring yourself to bring your beautiful strength into the fullness of abundance? Can you let the fear of scarcity fall away and embrace the richness of being and knowing that all is well? All is well brothers. All have enough. All will always have enough. Spread this wisdom with your words, with your heart, and insist that this be so. Take the beauty of your strong will and will that all have in abundance. Take the beauty of your strong body and make it so. Make it so for you. Touch your sphere of influence with the magnificent energy of abundance that you portray so well and teach all those you touch to do the same.

Stand tall and proud brothers, in this place of manifestation that is truly ours. Stand and create that which makes your heart sing and your spirit soar on wings that glow with love and delight.

Who are you man? What do you choose to create in a world of peace and life giving? Do you know how to create in a world of peace and life giving? Are you strong enough to learn what you do not know? Are you soft enough to teach what you do know?

Bring it forth then, your golden bough of wisdom. Bring it forth and give it as your gift into this physical world.

What do you know of life's sweetness? Speak it. Live it. What do you know of spirit's vastness? Speak it. Live it. What do you know of your heart? Speak it. Live it. Teach your sons and brothers, your fathers and friends what it is to be a heartful man dancing and playing in this amazing place. Claim your place as great, great grandfather to the men yet to come. Fill your place with the legacy you wish had been yours, and add a little more.

Release from your being any fears, any cautions, about your own power, your own strength. Trust yourself to be. Trust yourself to love. Embrace all of who you are and know that you are beauty.

On The Shore

Gendenwitha awoke to a soft dawn light that showed only shadows of the recent storm. She pushed her hands into the warm sand of the beach on which she had slept and gazed out over the sea that is the home of Ayizan, She Who Initiates Into Other Ways of Knowing and Being.

Her journey through Ayizan's home had been marked by many storms that stirred and boiled the waters to a depth she could not swim beyond. Some of the storms tossed her so wildly she felt as though she'd be torn limb from limb. Gendenwitha found herself many times swimming through the same place she had been the day before as some new storm blew in from the west and shoved her back toward the east where she had begun. Now and again a storm would come from the east and propel her rapidly toward the western shore before she'd even noticed the movement. But usually, she swam and swam and felt as though very little progress was being made.

When she found herself finally at the shore she'd worked so hard to reach, Gendenwitha was too tired to even rejoice, she simply lay down on the warm, dry sand and slept for a bit, or maybe more.

And then today came. To her east lay the home of Ayizan, the sea that had challenged every aspect of her will to live. To her west, Gendenwitha could see a row of mountains so covered with trees the ground was nowhere visible and so tall they surely kissed the stars at night. The mountains lay between her and there, and blocked her view of there, the place to which this journey would ultimately lead.

Gendenwitha smiled at the mountains, her eyes glittering with mischief and anticipation now that she was rested. "We shall become great friends, you and I," she whispered as she rose to her feet, kissed the sun in gratitude for a new day, and continued her journey toward.

MAN

Faunus stood at the gate, eyes sparkling eagerly, for today was his day to enter manhood. He had bedecked himself in his finest clothes and combed his hair into a shining braid in which he wove a string of stone beads; emerald for strength of body, sapphire for the gift of speech, ruby for his blazing passion, pearls and opals for the softness of love, gold for the pure light of spirit.

He'd prepared for this day for a long time and now, as the sun rose over the eastern hills, seven men walked softly toward him, they were his greeters. The first to reach Faunus was Atri, He Who Walks in Wisdom. His instructions to Faunus had taught him how to express his passionate spirit in ways that built unions with all who walked near him. Faunus gave Atri one eagle feather in gratitude for these teachings and followed the older man's lead to the ceremonial ground.

His greeters stood in a circle around Faunus, each choosing his place based on the attribute of manhood he represented for this new man. Outside of their circle stood a circle of all the other men in Faunus' life. Faunus, standing in the center of this ring of vibrant life, knew that he stood in the center of the creative force behind all life.

A drum's voice rose from the edge of the circle and the men began a slow, winding dance around Faunus, a dance that spoke of the inter-weaving of all beings and ended in the place where all are one. Faunus joined the dance as the rhythm picked up and it became about the quickening of a soul creating a body. He danced man's part in this act of welcoming souls to the physical plane, gracefully moving among and around the other dancers, allowing all to admire his beauty and strength. The men laughed together in this passionate dance, their feet meeting Earth's heart beat with every step. They danced themselves into union with all that is and blessed the land with their pearly fluid, feeding the soil with their fertile abundance.

After a time, the dancing slowed and Atri appeared at Faunus' side, eagle feather woven into his hair with many others. He fed Faunus a wheat cake for the sustenance of all his people, a strawberry for the sweetness of the heart, and a handful of grapes so Faunus would remember that for one to thrive, all must thrive.

Another greeter, Potos, stepped forward and gave Faunus a deep red garnet to remind him that a life full of desire is a life fully embraced.

Tannus came next to Faunus side and presented him with a drum, showing him how to build the beat so it sounded like thunder rolling in across the land. And with this gift, Faunus would remember to send his wisdom beyond his place of immediate contact.

When Zamba held out his hand to Faunus, on his palm lay a clay sculpture in a beautifully knitted lace wrap. These things Faunus received, knowing he lives to create beauty within the physical realm.

Kama, He of the Open Heart, embraced Faunus, enfolding him in the softness of pure love, thus ensuring that Faunus would always know when love was present.

Jolly Fu-Hsing then approached, laughter upon his berry stained lips as he peered at Faunus from beneath the brim of a ridiculous hat of ferns, bark, flowers and a pair of small balls. Faunus laughed when Fu-Hsing presented him with this absurd appearance and he knew the beauty of humor in all aspects of life.

Finally, Nataraja danced forward, winding his way through the gathered men to Faunus side, clapping out an uneven rhythm as he came. Nataraja stood facing Faunus for a long time, his rhythm of claps growing full then ebbing, moving in joyful light heartedness, then focused intensity, always, always, changing. And with this gift he taught Faunus that life is a dance of ever changing rhythms, all to be embraced.

The men joined together in more dance, feasting and laughter. They played until the moon began to greet the new day's sun, welcoming this new man into the fullness of his being.

Chaos

Come sisters; dance with me in this place between the worlds of flesh and spirit, this place that is woman's true homeland. We do, we always have, stood in this place that is neither fully flesh nor fully spirit. This place is, we are, the gate through which all must pass to cross from one side to the other.

I stand here freely, in the place that is inherently mine, organically mine, spiritually mine, ours. I stand with no protection other than myself and my birth right as woman. As I stand, so do you, sister.

The winds of spirit whip and blow, swirling around us, beyond us, through us. The sounds of spirit walk beside us, within us. The chorus of the great chaos, the womb of all life, resonates sweetly in the wombs of our bodies. Our bodies, these breasted and wombed garments, our bonds to the world of flesh, our gifts to the world of flesh. These bodies hum and vibrate with the intensely physical energy of the intensely physical world below our feet, within our hands.

Stand here freely sisters, in the place between the worlds where all life and all potential teem and swirl, seek and find. Balance in this place is our birthright. Balance in this place of greatest chaos is organically ours because we are the gate through which all must pass to cross from either side to the other.

Listen now to the call of Spirit, the sweet voice of all that is not flesh, all that seeks to be flesh, and all that has no such desire. Listen to the savory call of all the freedoms of the universe, of flying, of moving with the speed of thought. Listen to the call of shapeshifting, of knowing that which is not spoken, of seeing that which has no form. Walk to this side of this place between the worlds and feel the fresh winds of possibility, and the ancient winds of all knowing. Touch the breath of fire and know that it is good. Touch the breath of air and know that it is good. Watch, feel, fire and air dancing around and through one another, each transforming and each holding form. Know that all is well in this spirit place of greatest chaos.

Listen now to the call of body. The physical form that forms itself by condensing spirit into a compact shape who's many swirlings and sparkings are close enough together to be easily perceived by others in physical form. Listen to the sweet songs of all who remember they are spirit and all whose focus lies elsewhere. Feel the pullings of touch, of taste. Smell the goodness of damp earth, damp body, moistened for nourishment. Know the condensed physical forms of other spirits in body. Touch with your two hands the body called water and know that it is good. Touch with your two hands the body called Earth and know that it is good. Watch, feel, earth and water dance in and around and through one another, each transforming and each holding form. Know that all is well in this physical place of greatest chaos.

Return with me now to the place at the very center. The place where flesh and spirit are inseparable. Where they dance in and around and through one another. Where we dance in and around and through one another. We find our unity here. We find our diversity here. We find that we are part of all and we are not all. Here in this swirling, whirling vortex of all possibility we stand fearlessly for this is our home.

Sweep your arm in an arc over your head and watch the rainbow that follows in its path, the rainbow filled with life. Sweep your arm in an arc below your belly, your womb, and invite some of that life to pass through you, to birth through you.

Move your body. Dance to the rhythm of life in all its phases. Dance to the birth rhythm, dance to the death rhythm. Dance spirit, dance flesh. Ebb and flow, spark and rest. Breath the energy that is pure life into your heart until you remember in all parts of your being that you, woman, stand free, strong, and balanced at the center of the center of the chaos that is the birth place of all that is.

LAYING THE PATH

The souls who desire physical life gather to choose their journeys and Shai walks among them. He hears in his mind the many thoughts swirling about each soul, what each has done, what each would like to do and how they believe their desires can be manifest. This is a time of great creativity and Shai's aura flashes and sparkles with the inspiration surrounding him.

Notus speaks directly to Shai, telling of the desire to experience heat in its extremes, to know the parched taste of its dryness, the sweltering steam of its wetness, and the relief of its warmth in the face of cold.

Baiame also speaks to Shai, telling of a life full of intuition and playful mischief making. Coyote's many talks of the fun of learning by what is hidden rather than what is revealed, of walking backwards to the realities of those around oneself appeals to Baiame's sense of humor.

Baiame and Notus have been friends since before either can remember and for this journey they'd like to appear as brothers, born to a mother and father who can love the heat of one and the playful unpredictability of the other.

Shai smiles quietly at the way these mixed desires spark his imagination. These two, Notus and Baiame, have a way of presenting him with the most intriguing puzzles to piece together. And so Shai walks on among the gathered souls, listening for the two whose desires will complete the puzzle Notus and Baiame have given him. And he finds them, one who desires to experience life as a potter and to mother sons who are very different from one another. The other desires to father an energetic family and experience most of life as play.

Rubbing his hands together in excitement as he anticipates what these souls could do, Shai introduces them to one another and watches their auras flash and swirl, sparkling and changing colors as they weave their energies together to create a physical family.

****

Dana arrived on Earth first, born to the parents she chose and full of anticipation for her journey. Omacatl followed her quickly, anxious to grow into his full body. At birth, his smile lit the room and his parents welcomed him with laughter. He grew to adulthood filled with wonder at how deeply satisfying life on Earth could be.

Omacatl and Dana followed their paths to the place of meeting, prodded from time to time by reminders sent from Shai that encouraged one or the other to shift direction toward the meeting point. And when they met, each felt a distant echo of familiarity and neither, upon looking at the other, could imagine why. So they walked away.

Notus and Baiame watched for some time as their intended parents crisscrossed one another's paths, all the while managing to avoid another meeting. They had all agreed the youngest of the boys would be born in Dana's twenty-eighth year. Her twenty-seventh year came and went and still Dana and Omacatl had not fallen in love, or really even noticed one another. Shai watched calmly, knowing from long experience that the plans encounter unexpected changes once a soul crosses over. In Dana's twenty-eighth year, Baiame and Notus were born as twin brothers to Vasanti and they forgot all about Dana and Omacatl.

The boy's lives took shape as they had planned, happy and heated. Their growing awareness of life on Earth led them on many imaginary adventures into adulthood. And one day their mother died, and a week later her cousin Omacatl received another reminder from Shai of a part of his path he had not yet walked, he would now have two sons.

Notus and Baiame were not at all happy about this, they'd heard their mother speak of her cousin who laughed and played his way through life, but they'd never met him and they missed their mother terribly. Some members of their family thought it a bad decision on Vasanti's part to leave her beautiful twin boys to irresponsible Omacatl and they pleaded with her parents to make a different choice. Baiame and Notus' grandparents also questioned their daughter's choice of guardian but they had known her to be a good mother and she had been very insistent on Omacatl. They packed up their grandsons' belongings and prepared them for the journey to the distant home of this cousin their mother had admired.

Omacatl was quite surprised when news arrived that he would be father to the eight-year-old twins. What did he know of fathering? And what would this do to his lifestyle? He loved his cousin Vasanti and had talked with her often about her boys, but this he had not foreseen. After much thought and considerable discussion with friends, Omacatl knew in his heart that these boys would open his life to adventures he desired but had never dared hope for, and so agreed to welcome them as sons.

In the month before Notus and Baiame arrived, Omacatl's life was a flurry of transformation. He moved to a larger home so his sons would have room to play. He bought toys and furniture for their room and spent many hours re-arranging all of it so everything would look inviting and fun when they arrived. He inquired about their favorite foods and filled his kitchen with them. He even learned to cook after he realized that eight-year-old boys probably wouldn't know how to prepare their own meals.

When the day arrived, Baiame and Notus held anxiously to their grandma and grandpa's hands and an exhausted and excited Omacatl awaited the knock on his door. And the knock finally came. Omacatl opened his door to find his aunt and uncle and two wide eyed young boys who stared at him with a mixture of terror, sorrow, and just a hint of anticipation for a new adventure.

Their first year together, this family of three men, was one of discovery. Sometimes it was fun filled and sometimes angry or tear filled. And through it all their hearts wove together and they became sons and father.

Notus and Baiame loved having a father for the first time in their lives, and still they missed a mama. They talked often about their mother's soft lap, her gentle touch, her perfumes and the high sound of her laughter that was so different from Omacatl's deep tones. And they wished every time they saw a shooting star that they could have a mother again.

Omacatl also felt the lack of a mother for his sons and found himself looking at his lovers differently, wondering if any would like to love his boys as sons. One by one, he discovered they would not, mothering was not part of any of their desires. This really didn't surprise Omacatl, he'd chosen each of these lovers at times when fathering didn't appear to be part of his path. So he opened himself to a new lover who would like to mother Notus and Baiame and went on about his light hearted life.

Dana had grown quite skillful and well known as a potter. Her sculptures and vessels of clay were displayed in galleries in many different towns and she delighted in life. One day she decided to find a new home for herself, one with room for a larger studio and a yard for gardens. She received a little nudge from Shai in the form of a house just a few doors away from Omacatl's that was everything she wanted. Dana was so delighted with her new home that she started planting gardens immediately. And each day, she noticed the twin boys who ran by her house, laughing and chasing one another in various imaginary games. The boys made her laugh, bringing back memories of her own childhood, and she began speaking to them when they ran by.

Toward the end of summer, Notus and Baiame introduced their dad to Dana and announced their decision that she was the mother they wanted. Upon hearing that, Omacatl and Dana laughed, winked at each other, and told the boys it didn't work quite that way, but they'd see what the future might bring. Well of course the boys weren't going to leave that to chance, so they set about wishing on falling stars again , and Shai set about nudging Dana and Omacatl to remember their plans with these boys.

In Dana's thirty-eighth year, she and Omacatl made a family with Baiame and Notus. Dana began teaching Notus about the extremes of heat. He loved the kiln in her studio and she taught him how to bake fresh clay pieces into just the right finish for strong pots and sculptures. Baiame had already been learning Coyote's ways well from his father, who still laughed and played through life. And these beautiful twin boys grew into the fullness of their own paths under the loving eyes of their mother and father.

After many years passed, when Notus and Baiame were men with grown families of their own, each having lived lives full of fire and play, Omacatl woke from a dream one night and reached his hand across the bed to Dana. Her warmth soothed him back into a very deep sleep and he dreamed of a time before his birth when he and his beloved Dana and his sons had all planned this journey together.

FROM ALONE

Today was a day when inner struggle loomed large in Cerridwen's life. She had recently passed days of semi peace and a few weeks of blossoming hope. She had integrated many of the hard lessons of this initiation and the new lessons had appeared to be of a lighter nature.

But today, oh today, she awoke with the loneliness enveloping her bed, right where she'd left it when she fell asleep. She did what she'd learned to do, got out of bed, ate a good meal and went to a place where people who knew her were gathered. Cerridwen was too restless to stay long so she returned home, then left again several times before finally returning to bathe herself and wash away some of the layers of aloneness.

She let her tears and body oils blend with the water and carry away the scent of fear that had accumulated through her long day. Cerridwen breathed deeply onto the water and let out cries of rejection from the little girl who was so often teased for being different and was so often the last one asked to play. She reminded herself that she does know how to play, she's not all serious and wise and thoughtful and she doesn't have to live in that box just because others see her there. Cerridwen sighed deeply at that thought and sought ways to transform her pain about being seen so often as Priestess and so seldom as Ordinary Woman.

The thoughts transformed slowly, taking new shape as the whirls in the water took new shape and finally she remembered her power is in the now and best expressed actively. And Cerridwen knew then that she must invite herself out to play and touch her heart with others, that she must set aside the veil of Priestess at times and cease using that to separate herself from the people around her.

NINKARRAK'S JOURNEY

"I'm moving on. Going to a place where I can live in harmony, where all that is wrong here will not be." Ninkarrak stated this flatly as she packed the last of her belongings into traveling bags.

Gently laying her hand on Ninkarrak's arm, Hagia Sophia spoke to her heart. "And you will not mourn all that you leave behind granddaughter? Your family? Your friends? The food and sights and sounds, the ways of your birth place?"

"I will not." Ninkarrak responded. "The ways of this place sicken my soul, they sicken the souls of all humans."

"And will there be others in your new home, or will you be alone?" Hagia Sophia looked deep into Ninkarrak's eyes, searching her depths for the questions and fears she knew must be present.

"I'll find others along the way. There must be others who see as I do. We'll know one another when we meet." Ninkarrak felt Grandmother's probing and did not like it. She looked aside, pulling her thoughts away from Hagia Sophia's steady gaze. She knew well her own doubts, her own fears and wonderings. She knew well the wise old woman's desire to keep all who shared love together, in the same place and in frequent contact. She knew well that her journey was one of walking away from as much as walking toward.

The wisdom of Ninkarrak's people taught her to always walk toward, to always have her motivation be of a positive nature. Walking away from was seen as giving up, as leaving behind, as coming from a place of regret and pain, or fear. These were not valued qualities among her people. Yet Ninkarrak knew that, this time, she must walk away in order to even see what she might want to walk toward. And so, hefting her few belongings on her back, she kissed Hagia Sophia's soft old cheek, said farewell to the others she loved, and began her long journey away from.

Ninkarrak walked away from a way of being that encouraged difference and yet scorned all who were not the same. She walked away from a way of being that valued what humans made more highly than what spirit made. She walked on and on. Each day she passed another outpost of her people, another sign that demonstrated the rules and ways of their lives.

After many weeks of walking, Ninkarrak began to fear that she would not be able to walk far enough to reach the end of her people's influence and see clearly into another way of being. She made camp in a family of beech trees, interrupting her journey to rest and clear her mind.

Hagia Sophia's words came back to her and she thought about all she had left behind. She searched her mind for her own innocence, the part of her that had been able to disbelieve her growing awareness of how out of balance her people were. It was that innocence that allowed her to live among them as long as she did. She looked at her mind pictures of her mother, a woman who must surely have also seen the imbalances, sometime. A woman who acknowledged no such vision, but whose teaching had laid the foundation for Ninkarrak's ability to see. Shaking her head sadly, Ninkarrak whispered to the woman whose body she had been part of, sending energy to her so she too could break the mind bindings.

After several days of rest, several days of remembering why she journeyed away from, she picked up her traveling bags and walked again. Her path was still cluttered with the signs of her people, filled with the things that spoke to her of imbalance, of battling with spirit rather than living in spirit. Every now and again though, she'd notice a human being different than she'd seen before, she'd notice a flower, or bird, or four legged that she'd never seen. This didn't happen often, but when it did, she saw.

Ninkarrak's heart began to whisper to her of a different way to be human. She began to feel little, tiny, pieces of what she was journeying toward. With each tiny piece, she grew more determined to walk on to wherever it was she was going.

And then the rain began. The sky grew dark and the wind blew cold across her wet skin. She slept at night, huddled into the driest place she could find, listening to the steady, monotonous falling of the rain. All the other Earth Walkers that could had disappeared into dry places. Ninkarrak walked, and sat, and slept, alone in the rain for days and days. She cried with the sky, first for her cold, wet, muddy self, then for the ones she loved who could not journey to this place with her. She cried for the pain she felt when some among those she loved called her crazy for wanting this journey. She cried for those yet to be born, yet to grow up in the place she was leaving. She cried herself to sleep in the embrace of a fine old spruce tree and didn't wake again until the warm morning sun kissed her face. This day, she rose not knowing if her journey was good.

By making this journey, she walked away from the wisdoms of the old ones of her people. She walked away from most of what she knew about how to be human. The teachings of her people pressed hard upon her and she sat all day in the arms of the old spruce. She was afraid to leave her den. Afraid if she began to walk, she'd walk back to her people, or away from them.

Night sky rose, moon and stars glistening at her through the spruce needles, and Ninkarrak sighed with relief that another day had passed. She settled into sleep, searching night sky with her weary heart for visions of what she walked toward.

"Walking away from is not so different from walking toward," whispered Spruce to her sleeping guest. "Either will get you to a place where you are not. Either is something I cannot do at all." Ninkarrak responded with a stretch and continued her dreams. Hagia Sophia appeared, beckoning her to follow, calling to her senses with a bowl of her favorite, steamy, thick soup. "Are you sure this is not your home?" she asked. Ninkarrak rolled away, startling herself as Spruce's branches brushed against her arm. She awoke to hear herself saying, "It's not my home Grandmother! I love you, but it's not my home!"

In the morning, Ninkarrak walked away from Spruce on tired legs, journeying still further from the home that was not really home and the people who were her people, and yet she was not really one of them. Her heart was heavy and light at the same time and the morning passed quickly as she finished her thinking from the previous day.

Midday found Ninkarrak, the sun shining proudly above her, standing at the top of a hill. She looked into the valley below and saw the place she was walking toward. All the many kinds of Earth Walkers were in that valley, each going about their daily ways of being; talking, singing, and chirping merrily to all they came across. The waters ran clear and free, the trees very nearly danced on their roots with their joy of life. She could not hear one voice of anger, pain, or fear. She saw no acts of unkindness. She saw no places of sickness or need. She had found the place where all that was wrong among her people was not.

Ninkarrak ran down the hill whooping and laughing, she tumbled and somersaulted and danced her way to the valley, and stopped suddenly when she got there. In front of her stood only her grandmother, Hagia Sophia. All of the other Earth Walkers had disappeared, the dancing trees stood still, and she sat in silence. Way, way, off in the distance she could hear bursts of laughter and whooping, then sudden silences.

Ninkarrak stared at her grandmother, confused at both her presence and the absence of all she had seen from the hill. She had, afterall, walked for months away from where her people were, how could Grandmother have gotten here before her? How could she have gotten here at all?

Hagia Sophia looked deep into her granddaughter's eyes, a sparkle glinting in her own. "Every step you took brought you closer to my heart granddaughter. Do you really believe you're the first among us to know this place? No, little sister, we've dreamed it for a long, long time. My grandmother's grandmothers held this dream too. We've all passed it on as best we could. You, however, and the others of this time, are the first in many generations to find the way to this place. The ones you saw as you arrived all died or moved on long ago and this place has been waiting since. Do you hear the others of this time arriving?"

Ninkarrak nodded her head, indicating she heard but was still not ready to speak.

"Good then." Hagia Sophia breathed deeply and sat down beside Ninkarrak, "We will have to build our lives here. We know too much now about what can be to ever be happy in the old home again. All that is here for us is room to grow, and opportunity to live in balance. Each of us must make that balance happen or it will not be."

PEACE

Humans lived for many thousands of years in peace until a time came when there were so many of them that they had to live close to one another.

With the close living quarters came many arguments about how to live. The more they argued, the more groups they divided into. Some groups began competing with the others to birth more children, believing that eventually their group would outnumber the others and their way of life would become the way of life.

As their numbers grew, their arguments grew more hostile and they began making tools with which to kill those who lived differently. Of course, every Human lived differently from some other Human and some of them realized the tools might be used to destroy the entire tribe. They decided to overlook some of their differences and join together in large groups they called nations. They established rules that distinguished one nation from another by describing how the people of each nation were allowed to live.

Disagreements continued between the nations and then began appearing within each nation. They made more rules, trying to end the differences between themselves by leaving very little room for difference to exist. The rules began stealing the sense of freedom each Human needed to survive and many felt their spirits sicken and die.

The day dawned when wisdom came to some of the Humans. They began believing there could be other ways to live, ways that had no need for killing bodies or spirits to resolve differences. As their numbers grew, the Wise Ones became aware that they too could become simply another nation, overpowering those that lived different from themselves until their way of life became the way of life. This was not what they wanted. They sought an end to coercion in all forms. They thought about this, talked about this and tried as many new ways of being as they could imagine. Finally, they found a way they thought would work.

The Wise Ones chose to live among all the nations of Earth, claiming their whole tribe rather than a fraction of it. They chose to work openly to remove and prevent passage of rules that stifle freedom. They chose to work openly to prevent the killing of bodies or spirits over differences. They chose to work in private to return any new gifts of stifling energy to their sources. Working for many years, in many places across Earth's surface, the Wise Ones learned that ignoring the offerings of these stifling gifts was all that was needed to return the gifts to those who gave them.

The ones sending the gifts felt a growing discomfort. They became aware that their amount of space on Earth was no longer as large as it had been. They became aware that they were themselves living without freedom. They became increasingly frustrated and feared the death of their spirits. Anger arose among them at the ones who would not pay attention to their rules. They tried using tools to kill the others and found that using the old ways of resolving differences simply made their space more crowded. Their gifts were returning to them as fast as they sent them out and their frustration grew larger.

The day finally dawned when wisdom came to some of these frustrated ones, and they found doors that led to freedom. They joined in the work of the other Wise Ones and the spiral continued until all found their ways to freedom.

The mountains of frustration the Humans had created turned into iridescent mountains of breathtaking beauty that to this day commemorate the Human Tribe's reclaimed wisdom: peace prevails when each does as they will and harms none.

Gift

Prisni sat silent on a log, watching her winged relatives play joyfully with air and listening to their chorus of songs. She wished to make a gift to air. Air gave to her daily in the form of wind; blowing softly through her hair and about her body, moving the water so it licked the land and delighted her ears with sound. Sometimes it blew in great gusts and swept all in its path along to another place, rearranging her world and giving her new sights to explore. Air carried the winged ones she loved, and her dreams of being able to travel with them, wing to wind, unimpeded by the challenges of walking over and around.

Prisni pondered long and hard about how to gift air. She wanted to give something that was truly hers and she finally decided a thought would be a good gift.

She waited until a day when the wind was blowing from all directions, circling her home with a mighty storm. She went outside and stood at the center of the wind. Facing north Prisni thought of the wind as wisdom, facing east, as creative energy. She faced south and thought of physical endeavors and turning west thought of manifestation.

Confident in her gifts to air, Prisni stood waiting for a sign that they had been accepted. Wind blew and blew all around her, whipping her hair and scattering leaves, but there was no acknowledgment of her gift. She was puzzled. Many times she had watched the winged ones sing to air and have their gifts acknowledged immediately by a fresh gust or sudden stillness.

She called to air in her mind, sending thoughts in every direction and still there was no response. Perplexed, she turned to the east wind, the one she thought of as creative energy, and exhaled all the air from her lungs in one long, frustrated sigh....

The winds quieted immediately and a cloud floated down to her. On this cloud was a fine, strong old woman astride the back of a fine, strong, old tiger. Prisni was startled. She was looking for a response like the winged ones got, it was the only response from air she'd ever seen. With eyes wide she stared at the woman and tiger, making no sound, not even a tiny breath.

"Sister," said the old woman in a voice like rustling leaves, "I am Feng-P'o-P'o, some call me Kamikaze. I am the Divine Wind. I come to thank you for your gift. When you mingle your air with me that is truly a gift from you to me for your breath is yours alone and I am a being of air. Air is a substance of my life."

Feng-P'o-P'o blew gently on Prisni's face causing her to close her eyes and bask in the warm breath. She blew thoughts into Prisni's mind, gifting her in return with a substance of her life.

When Prisni opened her eyes again Feng-P'o-P'o and the tiger were gone. The storm had passed and the clearing around her home was silent except for her winged cousins who celebrated Prisni's friendship with air.

TRAIL IN THE FOREST

The path through the forest has twisted and turned, twining its way around trees, rocks and smaller growths of many sorts. The sun has risen higher in the sky on this walk, moving from the void of night's beauty, through dawn, and well into the late morning hours. Now approaching the fullness of noon, Iliani finds herself standing atop a boulder on the side of a tree-covered mountain. Valleys open out before her in all directions and the fullness of summer's foliage obscures the ground.

For today's walk Iliani has chosen to experience her journey fully open to those she will encounter and hawk is her first companion. Gliding silently on the high winds, hawk's shadow greeted Iliani as she stood looking at the valleys. Hawk settled on the boulder beside Iliani and began to shake the dust from her feathers, listening thoughtfully for the question she knew would come.

"How do I know the right path?" Iliani asked, her hands motioning out toward the dozens of valleys that looked pretty much alike.

Hawk cocked her head to the side, one dark eye observing Iliani closely, and then took flight, soaring higher and farther away until she disappeared from Iliani's sight.

Iliani chose a path, a trail cleared by deer, and began descending the hillside. She saw the trails of the forest dwellers crisscrossing one another and spreading out like spider webs beneath the green canopy of leaves. This woman of the forest knew to hold steady to a path or she'd find herself traveling in circles, so on she walked, carefully following her deer path and ignoring the voices of the other paths. The words of her grandmother whispered in Iliani's ears, "I could choose one path, follow it only, and walk so far on it that all I thought I knew at the beginning would completely disappear by the end. I could choose to follow a few steps on every path that crosses mine and walk always within an arm's length of where I began. I could choose to walk far enough on one path that I cannot see the place of beginning, then step onto another, and another after that and walk so far this way that I could never again find the beginning. And when the day is done, will I not have spent a whole day walking?"

A stream called to Iliani, beckoning her with the sound of cool water and when she stopped at its edge, frog appeared from among the grasses and sat staring at her.

"How do I know the right path?" Iliani asked again and frog regarded her for a long moment then slipped silently into the water.

Iliani sat on the sun-warmed rocks at the stream's edge, her body embraced by their heat. Soon, the warmth and the flowing water lulled her into a nap in which she dreamed of meeting a woodspirit.

"Surely you know all the paths here about," she said, "how do I know the right one?" The woodspirit laughed, plucked a very ordinary looking maple leaf from a tree and handed it to her.

"This is the trail marker," Iliani thought in the crystal clear haze of her dream. She slept awhile longer then awoke refreshed and certain she'd received her guidance. Picking herself up from the rock, Iliani looked around for a maple leaf and realized the forest was crowded with thousands of maple trees, each one a whole world in itself to some of the forest dwellers. She walked away from the stream, her question still hanging.

And so the day went until the sun set and the moon rose full. Iliani made camp then, settling herself for a night of deep sleep. As she lay, tree roots pushed against her body and bugs skittered and buzzed about her face. Soon it was apparent that sleep would not come. Iliani sat up in the moon light, back cradled by one of thousands of maple trees, and a single leaf fell at her feet. Her grandmother's chuckle teased at her ear again and Iliani laughed in return as her grandmother whispered, "If you enjoyed the day, you were on the right path."

RIDE THE RAINBOW

Hina, Woman of the Fluttering Butterfly Wings, Woman Who Rides the Rainbow to its Pot of Gold and Tickles Herself with its Brilliance, found herself sitting on a sticky log one day. She had worked very hard for many years to find this log. Of course, when Hina went in search of the log, she had no idea it was sticky. She always saw it as a soft, shining thing, a thing that would provide her with a place from which she could emerge with gleaming wings, soft skin, and eyes that glowed with excitement about every coming adventure.

Hina encountered many distractions and a few more than a few rough storms on her journey to find this special log. Several times she almost turned back, thinking this was not a right journey for her afterall. Each time, a voice inside her told Hina to keep going, to stretch her wings just a bit more and see if the log might be sitting just on the other edge of this time. So Hina flew on, her eyes always searching for her special log. Sometimes her wings would get so soggy or caked with mud from the rainy storms that she'd have to stop and rest until she'd regain her strength.

One time, Hina just thought she couldn't fly another inch and if she had to she'd surely die. She sat still on a beautiful flower, a dark blue Delphinium, for a long time, pondering her situation. As she pondered, Hina remembered her cocoon, that warm, safe place she'd lived before this journey began. She remembered that she could spin a cocoon and so she set about doing that. Hina spun and spun, she needed a very large cocoon for her full-grown body you know. When the cocoon was nearly finished, Hina crawled inside and closed up the opening behind her. She nestled into her new resting place and fell fast asleep.

While she slept Hina dreamed her tattered wings into good repair and her tired body into full vitality. When her dreaming ended, Hina stretched and yawned, in that half awake and half asleep place, and as she stretched she pushed against the sides of her cocoon and found it to be much too small for her rested body.

Hina was a bit disappointed with that awareness because it meant that yet another resting place wasn't quite right. She cried then, for a few moments, as she realized the journey would soon have to begin again. Her tears lulled Hina back into a light sleep and a gentle breeze rocked her cocoon, suspended lightly from the Delphinium stem. Hina could feel the breeze and found it pleasant. She could hear a very distant roll of thunder and dreamed that somewhere, on this pleasant summer afternoon, someone's gardens were being watered by a gentle rain that rinsed dust from leaves and flowers and returned it to the soil. When Hina's cocoon began jerking roughly in the wind, and thunder seemed to be pounding on the very center of her ears, she dreamed that her world was collapsing. She woke up frantic, afraid her cocoon would be ripped apart by this storm that was at least as big as any other she'd encountered on this journey. She also feared that her cocoon would stay intact and she'd feel cramped into this small place forever.

Hina breathed deeply to calm herself. She knew the storm would continue until it was done, regardless of anything she might do. She knew she must think with her imagination and find some way to get out of the cocoon without getting blown against a tree trunk by the raging wind. She stretched a bit again, very gently, and found the rain had softened the cocoon and the walls would give a little. Hina kept stretching and stretching, moving this way and that and trying everything she could think of to find a way to wiggle out of her cocoon.

Suddenly, Hina's cocoon dropped off the Delphinium stem and landed with a soft thunk on something hard that made a little tear in it. Hina pulled lightly at the little tear and peeked her head out to find the storm quieting down and herself to be sitting on a log. And indeed it looked to be a magnificent log. It had green paths of moss meandering along its crevices and ferns draping across it in lovely patterns. There were little holes where critters lived and places and places to explore.

This magnificent log lay beside a river that gurgled and played as it flowed along, promising Hina long, cool drinks and good places to clean the dust from her wings on dry summer days.

Hina walked along the log a bit and found its moss to be soft under her feet. She looked where the sun was beginning to stroke it and saw shining droplets from the recent rain, and she knew she'd finally found her log.

Hina stretched out on the log and listened to the life around her while the sun cleared the remaining storm clouds. She felt blessed many times over to have arrived at this place she'd searched the world for all these many years. After she was thoroughly warmed by the sun, Hina began to explore her log. She found it to be quite a lively place and she decided she'd live there for a long time to come. She knew that from this place she could do all she'd come this long way to do.

Hina continued quite happily for a while. She'd explore her log a bit, then stretch and fly a ways away to explore something else, always returning to the log to rest. One day when she returned home, the log had changed subtly. It felt a bit sticky and when she tried to fly away the next morning to explore that day, the log tried to hold her feet fast to its surface. Hina was quite surprised by this. Never before had that log appeared to be sticky at all. Hina relaxed her wings and began studying her log to see if she could figure this out. The stickiness got on her wings and try as she might, Hina could not lift them from it's surface without pulling long strings of sticky sap along that kept her wings attached to the log. Well, this was quite a dilemma and Hina thought about it long and hard. It wouldn't be so bad to just stay on the log, it was really a very nice place and she'd made friends with most of the others who lived there. There was plenty of food within easy reach and she could explore a bit. That sticky stuff wouldn't allow her to go as far away as she'd like, but of course, if she didn't fly so much, her wings wouldn't get so worn and her shoulders so tired and she'd have more energy to explore the log. Then again, there were the storms. If she couldn't leave her log, what would she do when the wind got big and the rains swelled the gurgling river until it became a roaring torrent?

After many days of pondering, crying, and searching for wisdom, Hina realized her log was getting stickier and stickier and she finally decided she could not continue to live on it. As much as she loved living on that log, she also needed to fly. Her wings were aching from lack of use, they were losing their brilliant colors, and she could hardly look at them without crying.

The day arrived for Hina to leave and she found that the sticky sap had covered a large part of her once lovely wings. She pulled her feet free of the sap, then took her best scissors and carefully trimmed away the parts of her wings that were stuck to the log. She cried and cried as she trimmed her wings, partly because it hurt so and partly because she was leaving parts of herself that had been beautiful in a place that had been beautiful and both were now turned sticky from sap that oozed out of secret places she hadn't known were there.

When Hina finished trimming her wings, she ran and hopped and tried to fly and ran and hopped away from the log that had once been her beautiful resting place. Hina cried and cried. Every time she remembered her wings she cried. Every time she remembered her log she cried. Every time she looked for her future, Hina cried. Her wings no longer felt strong enough or big enough to take her anywhere. Her feet still had sticky sap on them and now and again would threaten to hold her fast in a place she did not like.

Hina knew her wings would grow back and the sand she ran through would eventually clean her feet, but she didn't know when and she didn't know how long she could survive without resting. If only her log had truly been as she'd perceived it to be, Hina thought, she could be soaring through the air now instead of trudging and hopping along on the ground like some wounded creature who'd never ridden a rainbow to its pot of gold.

Then Hina got angry at her log until she realized it was only doing what logs do, seeping sap when their bark is broken. Then she got angry at the little bugs that ate through the bark and made her log seep sap. Then she got angry at the storms that made her tired so that she needed a resting place. Then she remembered that somewhere, sometime, she'd flown with small wings. Before her big wings grew, her small wings had carried her well.

Hina wasn't too sure small wings would work anymore; her body was afterall, bigger than the last time she'd had small wings. But then again, these small wings were a bit bigger than those too. So Hina stretched her wings and flapped them a bit and found that, weak as they were, she could lift herself a few inches off the ground with them and fly a few feet before she had to rest again.

Because she couldn't fly so well, Hina had to spend a lot more time than she used to finding food and safe places to sleep and that left her with very little energy with which to practice flying. But Hina remembered that she left her log because she needed to fly and if she couldn't learn to fly again it would mean she'd left her log for no reason. So, she squeezed in a few minutes of practice every chance she got. She'd practice flying and then remember why her wings weren't whole, so she'd stop and cry a bit and then she'd practice some more.

Hina could feel her wings getting stronger and stronger, but they still wouldn't carry her very far until finally, on a rainy day that started out to be most unremarkable, Hina stretched her wings for practice and suddenly found herself riding the arc of a rainbow and tickling herself with its brilliance. She smiled with delight at her beautiful new wings, the ones that flowed out from the heart of her old wings. And Hina knew again that she truly was Woman of Fluttering Butterfly Wings Who Rides the Rainbow to its Pot of Gold and Tickles Herself with its Brilliance.

NORTH SEA

Ran stirred the waves of the mighty North Sea, bringing forth from its depths the memories of many generations of beings. The waves washed in hungry leaps all along the shores and left behind them traces of lives gone before. The people living on the edges of the North Sea looked on in awe, it had been many generations since Ran made her wild side known to this depth. The songs of Ran's daughters could be heard over the steady beat of waves on once dry land. Their songs beckoned all, "Come forth! Come swim in this place of old memories!"

Many people moved inland, away from Ran's display of passion. Some stayed close to her side, listening daily to her daughter's songs and walking by night into the dream land of spirit, trying to discern the messages of this grand display. And they saw they had developed a fear filled respect for Ran and her daughters and felt it unwise for any to embark on a sea voyage without first gifting Ran to obtain her cooperation.

Ran's passionate display continued, calling daily for the people to open their hearts to her true message. She sprinkled the wisdom over their bodies in the mist of crashing waves, and she and her nine daughters sang it into their ears on the howling winds. The people listened but did not hear clearly. One or two at a time, they began walking the shore and picking up pieces of debris left in the wakes of the waves. Nightly they gathered around fires and told stories of the things they had found that day. They told of people and times gone by, of hearts woven together and broken apart. Stories were told of dreams realized and those not yet come to fullness. And one day, Erik found a gold earring lying on a stone in a small puddle of salty water. He remembered well the one who wore that gold for he had loved her many years past and grieved mightily when she failed to return from a journey. Erik sat on the rock for a long time and cried, a lifetime of questions and fears dissolving from his heart, and then he returned to his fire, gold earring in hand.

When he began to speak, the others around the fire listened with half ears and very little heart. They knew Erik as one of anger and unpredictable moods. He lashed out at many of them through the years, his angry words reminding them all of Ran's vicious storms.

"I believed she found me unworthy and so I was afraid to love again," Erik choked out between tears, holding the gold earring up for all to see. "Today, as I grieved anew for this lost love, I listened to Ran's heart. I listened to her daughters as they sang and I remembered that we are the great sea. We are Ran and all her daughters. If we are to calm this sea that has claimed so many lives, we must gift ourselves with our own hearts. Our gifts to Ran have been many and she throws them back to us and goes on storming. She never wanted those gifts. She and her daughters sing to us of the beauty of the open, unfettered heart and we've come to believe their songs are of anger and the fears of generations of our dead. Our guarded hearts, our fears of losing yet one more loved one, have twisted our vision and we now see an unfettered heart as something that's too wild and must be feared." Erik sat silent then, his message delivered.

Marya spoke next, her eyes dancing in the fire's light as she held up a silver box studded with red jewels. "I sat today at Ran's side, holding this box and trying to know whose hands had touched it before mine, and by whose act it came to be in the sea. I could hear all nine of Ran's daughters singing an alluring tune and my strongest desire was to follow their song into the sea. I sat awhile longer and then I heard her message too. Ran told me that a heart wary of being hurt is not a true part of our souls. We fight against one form of bondage by creating another. We fear that deceit by others will carry us to our ruin when in truth we deceive ourselves by believing we are any less safe and free than is the North Sea."

Marya sat silent then too, watching the faces illumined by the fire. The North Sea danced wildly beside them, Ran and her daughters all singing at once for the people to see. And all the people watched and soon they began to notice the waves, that were no less turbulent than before, looked like playful acrobats curling their toes in joyful leaps. The howling wind carried many tones that touched their bodies in delightful ways. And those terrifying surges of water running onto once dry land sounded like a hundred thirsty puppies lapping eagerly at a pond. And the people noticed their hearts. A light feeling swelled up within each and they knew Ran's reign of terror for what it truly was, their own hearts raging to be set free of all fears.

DANCING LOVE

Nammu, woman who feels her emotions to the very depth of the ocean of her being, sat teary eyed one day as she watched the woman she embraced as her heartsong dance away from her, her back turned to Nammu as her eyes rested on the distant horizon. Nammu felt as though Calafia, woman whose passion is exploring life, her heartsong, saw her as an impediment to her freedom and Nammu wanted only to have Calafia's eyes sparkle with delight again as she looked upon Nammu. She never wanted to impede Calafia's freedom; she celebrated the wildness of this woman whose soul would not be tamed. Nammu opened her mouth to speak her truth, to tell Calafia that all she wanted was to be smiled upon and delighted in during the times they came together, but the words would not come because so many tears lay on top of them.

Nammu was on her own journey to freedom; one that had begun with the sudden collapse of her old world and her grieving was long and hard. She wished for Calafia's embrace during her darkest times and found that Calafia could feel compassion but could also feel her pain so deeply that she could not embrace Nammu without damaging herself. Nammu, having lost most of her friends in the collapse of her old world, found herself sitting more alone than at any other time in her life.

She tried to comfort herself and found that her ability to cry seemed endless and she grew very tired of it. As Nammu grew more tired, Calafia's eyes rested more often on the distant horizon. Nammu came to a place one day of feeling the energy between herself and Calafia fade to a mere wisp. This energy that had once been so strong and vital was being suffocated and Nammu was not certain why.

She dived deep into the chasm between them and grabbed a handful of something that lay heavy over the once beautiful energy. Nammu pulled the thing out to the light and found it was huge chunk of her grief, raw and throbbing, not yet begun to heal. She touched the grief and quickly pulled her hand away because it was so hot.

Nammu laid the chunk of grief to the side and looked to see what else was lying on the once beautiful energy. She could feel something there but could not see it clearly and could not pull it loose. She realized then that what was there must be something of Calafia's.

She sat a long time and contemplated the piece of grief she'd pulled loose. She thought and thought about how to heal it in a way that would be complete. As Nammu thought, so did Calafia, though they mostly thought in silence because so many tears lay on top of their words.

A day came when Calafia announced she was walking to that distant horizon. She told Nammu she could come on part of the journey with her, but there would be many places where Nammu would not be welcome.

Nammu reached to one side to steady herself and try to stop the tears, and in doing this, she put her hand square on that hot piece of grief and it burned until she could not release it from her hand. Nammu knew then that this piece of grief was the part of her old world that still existed. More than anything else, Nammu craved a resting place; a place where time would stand still and change would cease for just one night so she could sleep deeply.

As she looked from her burning hand to Calafia's determined face, and back again, Nammu knew that in the burning was a warm familiarity where she had once rested, and she made a decision to seek a resting place in that warmth again.

Nammu told Calafia of her decision to return to her old world and Calafia responded with pain, this was the one choice Nammu could make that would pierce her heart the deepest. Nammu ran as quickly as she could to the piece of her old world that still was. A deeper pain settled over the once beautiful energy that still flowed between the two heartsongs. They tried to speak through it and around it and could barely whisper to one another over the roar of pain.

Nammu, upon sitting in what was left of her world but a short time, realized she had not come back to rest there but had returned to finish leaving there. She worked her endings as quickly as she could, and finally free of the grieving, left the old world behind for good and set out in search of the rest of her new world. Her heart was less than light as Nammu returned to the new world because she could feel Calafia's back turned to her. She knew that on top of her own old pain, Calafia now carried the fresh pain of Nammu's return to her old world.

Knowing she had only done what she needed didn't lessen Nammu's regret about the new pain Calafia carried because of her actions. She thought of talking to Calafia and sensed a silence that resonated to the depths of the ocean of Nammu's being and she decided that talking would only lead to more turning away.

Nammu knew that, if Calafia must turn away, she must release her gently and lovingly for it would do no good to try to hold her. Nammu cried again, cried tears that came from the place inside her that only Calafia had touched. She reminded herself that she did not know that Calafia would never come back, she had not said that. She remembered that all she really knew about Calafia's current thinking was that she was not here now. Nammu searched for comfort in that thought and found very little there to ease her mind.

Calafia had requested a period of no talk about their relationship and Nammu tried hard to honor that. She knew that Calafia's way of healing herself was to withdraw into her own sacredness and not return until she was whole. Nammu's way was to reach out to the one who shared the pain and try to talk and touch hearts to find the way to healing.

Nammu valued Calafia's way as much as her own so she looked for a middle ground by reaching through writing instead of speaking. Each time Nammu would share a piece of her truth with Calafia, and Calafia would respond with silence, she would cry again, cry tears of fear that in speaking her truth she was pushing Calafia further away. Nammu tried to walk outside of fear, and some days she did it well, and other days, she fell into its stickiness as Calafia's silence lingered.

Finally, Nammu came to a place of knowing that she had said all she could to Calafia, and from here, Calafia must be left to discern her own truth. Nammu set about preparing herself for whatever possible decision Calafia might embrace.

She looked within herself and knew that her love for Calafia ran very deep. She knew her pain could run as deep as her love if she interpreted Calafia's adventures and turning away as rejection of herself. Should they continue on, Nammu would have to heal the part of herself that saw rejection. Should they go no further, Nammu would have to heal the part of herself that saw rejection. Nammu chose to create her healing, to strengthen herself from within. She embraced Calafia by letting go of her and simply allowing what was beautiful between them to remain open so Calafia could return someday if she chose.

FEAR

"When the fear comes up, push your energy out through your heart and make your aura bigger and gentler." Yama said quietly, gently searching the depths of Eir's clear blue eyes with his own.

Eir returned his gaze with many questions in her eyes, trying hard to figure a way to word them that would not allow Yama to take her fears away from her.

"What is the purpose of fear Yama?" Eir finally said. "Why would we create such a trickster within ourselves?" Satisfied that she had worded this question so that Yama couldn't discount the value of fear, Eir sat quietly looking at this man who sought to teach her the ways of spirit. Or was it she who sought his teachings? She thought both were true, but couldn't be sure. As with so much of what transpired between herself and Yama, this teaching unsettled Eir to the core and she feared that if she allowed herself to think as Yama suggested, she'd be letting go of whatever kept her safe in truly dangerous situations.

"The purpose of fear?" Yama thought for a moment, pushing the laughter away from his eyes so Eir would listen rather than further defend her attachment to fear. "Why, I suppose fear is useful in shrinking your world when it's gotten so big you'll need to learn new skills to maintain balance. I suppose it could also be useful if you wanted to experience yourself as a closed and rigid being. Or perhaps fear could be used to perceive a threat to your body. Perhaps fear is not a trickster but teaches very straight forward lessons." Yama looked straight ahead, allowing Eir the privacy to take his words in unobserved.

"Fear has warned me well all my life." Eir responded. "I've released a lot of my fears as I've grown and learned to walk wisely in complex situations." Her arms lay across the table top between them, relaxed yet ready to move to a safer position if needed. Eir noticed the tension in her body that always accompanied fear, that alertness to move, dodge, cover herself should the assault continue. "Assault," Eir thought to herself, "I'm having a conversation with a good and proven friend, why would I even think this an assault?"

"And so you have." Yama agreed, "And with each fear you've released, what has the common lesson been?"

Eir thought for a moment, knowing she was about to admit to her own lack of conciousness and feeling her resistance to being seen that way. "The common lesson has been that whatever the fear was, heeding it kept me from seeing from a different perspective than I was accustomed to."

"And did the fear ever keep you safe? Did your fear ever keep that which you feared from occurring?" Yama, still not looking into Eir's eyes, posed these questions gently.

"No," Eir responded. "It has alerted me though, so that I knew to not participate."

"Yes, that would be true. Could you not have gained those insights also by simply being fully aware of yourself and those around you?" Yama fell silent, giving Eir time to feel the difference between fear and awareness. "Perhaps fear's true purpose is to alert us to the challenges we've create for ourselves by failing to notice or act upon our earlier awareness. And perhaps the path of wisdom when faced with fear is to discern what to do, how to grow yourself big enough to gracefully handle the challenges you've created."

"But what if I can't? What if my dreams take me to places where I let other people down?" Eir asked.

"That's one of the challenges." Yama responded.

"What if I fool myself into thinking something's right when it isn't? What if..." Eir was preparing to let fly her whole string of defenses for fear.

"Those are all the challenges Eir," Yama took her hand in his. "Do you not see the way fear keeps you from trying? The way your attachment to fear as a guardian keeps you from finding out what's really possible as opposed to what you or those around you believe is possible? Fear always serves the same purpose, regardless of what you're fearing. It always says 'no' to experiences."

"But there are some experiences I choose not to have!" Eir's defense grew more passionate as she saw the edges blurring between desirable and undesirable experiences. As she felt her mind moving to the place where she knew all experiences are simply energy dynamics and there is no judgment of good or bad, that place where beliefs about right and wrong, pain and pleasure, success and failure are simply not relevant. That place; where sorting reality from fantasy was impossible without the framework of beliefs. Eir felt herself drawn into this place, and then pull away from it, afraid she'd lose her sense of social responsibility and become what she most disliked, a person who took on responsibilities and then didn't fulfill them. A person who took on life and then didn't fulfill her potential.

Eir stopped at that thought and turned it over carefully, examining it from many sides. Yes, that was it, that was the fear at the bottom of all of her fears, the one she guarded so vehemently. "And how," she wondered, "Could I ever discover my potential if I'm afraid to experience what sits in front of me?"

"When the fear comes up, push your energy out through your heart and make your aura bigger and gentler." Yama said quietly. "Deep satisfaction with life comes only through embracing all of life with your heart."

STORYTELLER

The velvet blackness of night sky spread endlessly across the horizon as young Purutabbui sat at the edge of the forest that is his home. His time this night was being spent in meditation for he'd accepted the task of sorting through the wisdom of many generations of his people. He was to determine which of the old stories held value as history only and which were of value to now and the future. So many generations of his people had walked this same land that stories were piled deeper than the tallest trees and there simply were not enough story tellers to remember them all.

Purutabbui's first concern was in knowing what to do with the stories that were only for the past once he identified them. They did afterall tell where his people had walked and who they'd been. As such, they were honored the same as any elder would be. It was surely going to be a long night for Sun would not rise again until his task was done. Purutabbui turned a corner of his mind loose to work on the placement of the old stories while he focused the rest of his attention on the sorting.

He looked first at the contents of each story he knew and asked the question, "Does this speak of a life filled with greater love and harmony than we now know?" If it did, he knew the story contained teachings that had not yet been mastered and it must be told again. All of those stories he lay on the ground beside a fine cedar tree, and they made quite a pile.

All of the other stories, those that told of teachings mastered by other generations, he lay on the ground beneath a fine oak tree. Many voices had told these stories and echoes of those voices whispered in Purutabbui's ears, questioning what would become of their legacy. Purutabbui knew that if these ones were forgotten, eventually the lessons would have to be learned again, yet if they were held close, eventually there would be no room for new teachings.

"How to see through the darkness of this question?" he asked, searching the black velvet sky above him. "If I could see through you, lovely night sky, I could see through this question." And he fell asleep, the young man seeking to sort through the wisdom of many generations. He fell asleep to his question and awoke to a still dark sky that was lit only by distant flashes of lightening. The lightening spread its scent across the air and took Purutabbui's mind to another time, a time when the old story teller known now simply as The Way Seer, was teaching another how to discern teachings in a story that appeared to be only for entertainment.

"There will be a tiny spark," The Way Seer's coarse voice said, "it will feel inside of you like the spark off a piece of flint. The spark itself is not what matters, for it is only the manifestation of a point of contact. What matters is what the spark touches after it leaves the flint."

Purutabbui held that thought and returned his gaze to the lightening, watching intently as a bolt struck a nearby rock and sent sparks flying in all directions. "If each story were a spark," thought Purutabbui, "I could toss the sparks into the night sky and light the way through its darkness."

He rose then and walked to the pile of stories beneath the fine oak tree and one by one, tossed them to the lightening as it flashed. Purutabbui stood, tossing stories whose lessons were mastered, far into the night. And when he had finished, the velvety night sky glistened with endless stars, each the spark of an old story.

When morning dawned, Purutabbui called together all the storytellers of his people and gave them the pile of stories for now and the future. He told them each that the old stories now lived in the sky and could be told again at any time simply by touching one of the sparks of light in the night sky.

And so the stars were born and the minds of the people were freed from carrying the lessons of the past so they could fully embrace what was yet to come.

ZORYA AND WINTER FOX

Once upon a time, maybe long, long ago, or maybe yet to come, a village of women lived in the forest.

The forest was magnificent, filled with trees so large three women could barely touch fingers around their girth, and trees so small, a single hand could easily hug an entire trunk. Hundreds of birds filled the forest with their songs, so many in fact, that sometimes the women covered their ears just so they could hear their own thoughts.

Four leggeds walked the forest silently. Occasionally one would reveal herself to a woman walking alone. If the woman acknowledged her with a proper greeting, the four legged would join her and they would learn from one another for awhile. This brings us to the story of Zorya Vechernyaya and Winter Fox.

Zorya loved to walk this great northern forest at dusk. Just as the sun was preparing to set, she would finish her work and disappear into the forest. Now, Zorya was neither the oldest nor the youngest, the funniest, nor the most serious woman in the village. She was in fact, quite ordinary as the village women went. But then this was a village of ordinary women who all knew how extraordinary all women are. And so, her daily ventures into the forest were noticed. The other women wondered among themselves about what it could be that drew Zorya to the forest everyday at the same time. They all loved the forest and walked with her often, but none so often as Zorya.

One special day, Winter Solstice, Zorya left the village particularly early for her walk, which surprised no one because they all knew this was the shortest day of the year. This day though, Zorya had not returned by the time Grandma Moon sat high over the village and her sisters began to worry. It was unlike Zorya to miss a celebration and one was about to begin to honor the balancing of night and day.

The women decided all that could be done was to go in search of Zorya. They planned to slip noiselessly through the forest until they found her. And so, decorated in their most brilliant jewelry and clothing, for they were all prepared to celebrate Solstice, fifty women disappeared into the forest and the village became quiet and dark except for a cooking fire and the two very old women and one very young woman sitting beside it.

"They'll not find Zorya soon," said one of the old ones.

"Hmph," said the other as she lay a bit of bread close to the fire to warm.

"She's out there dancing with fox tonight. I've felt her doing that before," said the first.

"Dancing with fox?" said the young one, amazement on her tiny face, "Women don't dance with fox. Fox doesn't dance as we do!" She tried to imagine Zorya and fox dancing together and the picture in her mind was so silly it made her laugh. She was sure the old ones were trying to fool her so she'd learn something new, they did that often, you know.

The old women looked at one another and smiled.

"Not all women dance with fox, and not all foxes dance with women, but there is one near here who does, you'll see," said the first.

"Hmph," said the other, handing the young woman the now warm bread.

Quiet settled over the village again as the three listened to the forest for signs of their sisters.

****

The women searching for Zorya had looked in all the usual places for her and found no one other than a small rabbit who hurried away. The forest was unusually quiet and deserted except for a distant thumping that sounded a lot like their village drums echoing through the trees, but it was coming from the wrong direction. Cautiously, the women moved toward the sound, following it through trees and brambles, up hill and down for a long, long time until they found themselves in a part of the forest that few had ever seen.

The few who had seen this place began to smile and laugh, "Here we'll find Zorya," they all said. The others wondered how they knew and why they laughed, but kept their questions silent. They had walked far, in clothing meant for ceremony, not forest travel, and they were tired and more than a little angry at the thought of finding Zorya in a situation that might be fun.

"Here it is!" a woman called, pointing to a large vine that burst into bloom at her touch. "We follow this vine and we'll find Zorya."

Sure enough, a short way along the trail marked by the vine, there stood Zorya Vechernyaya, a broad smile on her face and an air of delight all around her.

Well, this was about enough for some of the women. That big smile on Zorya's face could only mean one thing, they'd spent most of a celebration night traipsing through the forest, catching their best clothes on brambles to find a woman who had dreamed so much in her walking that she'd forgotten her sisters would grow concerned at her unusual absence. A woman stepped forward, clouds of annoyance crossing her face as she prepared to confront Zorya. Zorya quickly put a finger to her lips and motioned all the women to her side.

"I followed my vision," Zorya said, "Winter Fox kept dancing in front of me, in my path. She'd beckon me to follow, and today I did. We walked and ran and danced in circles until all the other forest folks followed us here. You're the last to arrive. Look!"

Zorya pointed to another path and motioned for her sisters to follow. The women soon found themselves in the ceremonial circle of their own village where also were gathered all the other forest folks. In the center of them all sat a huge golden orb, a huge silver orb, two very old women and one very young woman. The air was warm like summer and cold like a winter night. The circle was bright as noon on a summer day and dark as midnight in a snowstorm. Zorya led the women in a dance around the golden orb, around the silver orb, and finally to their place in the circle of all the forest folks.

One of the very old women arose and picked up the two huge orbs as though they were feather light. Stretching her arms out and upward, she held the orbs in perfect balance and slowly turned so that each, the silver and the gold, shown brilliantly on all present.

"On this important night, " she began in her voice of wisdom, "we honor the power and beauty of all that is done in darkness. On this night of change, we honor the dreamtime. On this longest night, we honor Grandma Moon, Sister Sun, and Mother Earth by honoring one another."

Raising the orbs higher, she let out a wild yell and sang the Solstice chant:

> "The balance is here between day and night,
> We honor the dark as we honor the light.
> All walk in darkness,
> All walk in light,
> The journey is life that we honor this night."

She tossed the two orbs into the sky and watched as they danced around one another before settling into their places above the circle.

Reaching her hand to the other very old woman, she began to dance, slowly at first, enticing her friend to join her. The two swayed and whirled wildly for a long time, touching all in the circle before they finished.

The second old woman suddenly let her cloak slide away, revealing her thick coat of winter red fur and the long bushy tail that had beckoned all to this ceremony. And one very young woman and many much older than her, stared in amazement at Winter Fox.

"Hmph," said Winter Fox, gently patting the very young woman's head, "so I don't dance as women do?"

Lover's Journey

Kupala had danced among these hills and played often in these rivers as a boy. He stood now, a young man, looking at this land that had been his play ground, his place of learning and he loved all he saw. Echoing from the mountains he could hear the voice of his lover, Ataksak, calling to him. Kupala and Ataksak had not yet met, except in spirit, and today Kupala would begin the journey to Ataksak's side.

When he came of age, one of the old ones in Kupala's village had journeyed with spirit to help him find a mate. All were pleased when the other's spirit answered from the frozen mountains of the far north. A very strong spirit was needed to attract a mate over such a distance. And so Kupala's journey began. He traveled alone for most of the journey, taking with him fine gifts for his new relatives, items and ways of seeing the world that were highly valued by his people. On the journey he took himself deep within and sorted through his life up to this point, wrapping himself in his fondest memories of his people. And all the while he wondered about Ataksak. Who was this one who called to him from so far?

When Kupala was a short distance from Ataksak's village he made camp in an obvious place and waited for one of the people to invite him into the village. On the second day a young woman approached and upon hearing he had come to mate with Ataksak, she laughed, hugged him and told him to follow her quickly.

Ataksak was much loved in his village and as news spread that his mate approached, the people put on their finest clothes and began preparing a feast. Ataksak's father helped him prepare to greet Kupala with all the honor deserved by a new mate. A blanket of deep red, blue, and green was spread on the ground at Ataksak's door. In the center were two soft cushions, a tray of delicious smelling foods and a gift for

Kupala. Ataksak took his place on one of the cushions and awaited Kupala's entrance into the village.

The old ones of the village lovingly escorted Kupala to Ataksak's home. And there sat Ataksak, wearing his finest clothes, his black hair gleaming in the sun, his dark eyes wide, eager to see this one called Kupala. And he smiled deeply upon seeing Kupala's handsome features and strong body. Kupala too, appraised his new mate on this first meeting. Ataksak's dark features and strong body appealed to him, but even more, the soul looking at him through Ataksak's eyes was indeed the one he recognized as his mate.

The men stepped toward one another, smiles playing across their faces, and began a slow, circling dance that wound through the people surrounding them. And with each step they watched one another's movements and expressions until their dance brought them to the cushions centered on the blanket at the door of their new home.

Kupala seated himself facing Ataksak, took hold of Ataksak's hands and looking into the depths of his eyes, allowed their souls to embrace. Ataksak opened his heart to Kupala and knew this man's soul as he knew his own. And in that moment these two and all around them saw that this journey of love was the continuation of one begun lifetimes ago.

Visions

Vision Quest

"And when it all ends, what do you suppose will happen next?" Prometheus, He Who Foresees, asked of the people sitting with him.

Of late, Earth had been acting strangely. Seasons were just a bit off from what they used to be. Earthquakes, volcanoes and violent storms seemed to be happening more frequently. The people's emotions were odd and they seemed unable to keep a hold of their own lives. They were caught up in whirlwinds of change that came out of nowhere.

Many were confused and sought answers in whatever forms they could find. Some pretended nothing was different, some numbing themselves, some seeking greater knowledge, and some simply turning in circles of confusion. All lived with the question, "What is it? What's happening in our times?"

Prometheus sat silent, waiting patiently for an answer to his question.

"Rest," answered one.

"Wisdom," said another.

"Something new," said a third.

"And if you're resting, what will that be?" Yetl questioned from somewhere in the group. "And if you're wise, how will you be? If you're doing something new, what will you do?"

Yetl returned to silence and waited, touching his mind with that of each person present, and with those who were there but appeared not present. He opened himself to receive the thoughts they would share about what will come next.

Yetl saw many visions, some of peace, some of confusion. Some thoughts were of fear and others of love. He waited quietly as the people's thoughts wove together into a brilliant tapestry and came to life. He touched the minds of the people again and sent them visions of this tapestry; its threads vibrant with color and woven gently together in a way that lovingly embraced each within its wholeness.

Prometheus questioned again, "and when it all ends, what do you suppose will happen next?"

And the people, one by one, then together in their wholeness, those who were present, and those who were there but appeared not present, joined with Yetl and raised the vibrant tapestry of their visions out of their hearts and into their lives.

THE END TIMES

Hours and days spread in a vast arc behind Kefa as she tirelessly walks toward the setting sun. Time, her legacy, stands before and behind Kefa wherever she goes. She enjoys time, it helps her see where she's been and how long it will be until she arrives at her destination. Kefa's destination is the end of time and she alone knows when her play with time will reach its fullness and come to an end.

As Kefa walks with time, so do all others with curiosity about linear movement – the thought form that marks where one is by seeing where one has been compared to the destination sought.

Unlike the others who walk with her, Kefa has mastered many of time's lessons and knows how to grow both old and young. She knows how to coax time into being a playmate, stretching short hours into long ones and then shortening again when she chooses to move quickly through experiences. Kefa demonstrates these skills to all who watch her.

As Kefa continues her walk toward the setting sun, she begins to notice repetitions in her experiences and she knows that her walk with time is drawing to an end. She's almost learned all there is to know by walking in linear thought and will soon find knowledge of other sorts to explore.

She looks about herself and sees many linear experiences in which she has not yet played. She calls them close to her and coaxes time into shortening so she can play in all of these experiences before her new journey begins.

The others walking with her are startled by the speed of time as Kefa moves into the fullness of its momentum. They find themselves confused and unable to integrate the new experiences as quickly as they're having them. Many of them seek Kefa's advice, some seeking knowledge of how to integrate more quickly, some seeking knowledge of how to slow time again.

Kefa answers their questions with increased speed as her journey to the end of time approaches its goal. She holds out her hand to those who seek to integrate more quickly and beckons them to join her on the journey beyond time to whatever comes next.

To those who seek to slow time again, she joyfully gives them the gift of time as she and the others reach the end of the wisdom of time and burst into the wisdom of being.

WEAVER

Spider Grandmother, Weaver of Earth, gifted Human Woman with her own ability to take nothingness and weave it into life. She taught her to sing as her weaving progressed, to instill joy in the creation she wove. She gave Human Woman threads of many colors and textures, telling her to mix together what pleased her heart and eye.

Human Woman wove many creations, each different from the others. She wove some into beingness right away, some she wove awhile, then unraveled and began again. She started to see the threads as her own thoughts and understood that all she thought, she could bring into being.

Through her weaving, Human Woman began to understand her power to create and asked Spider Grandmother for other tools with which to work. Spider Grandmother gifted Human Woman with the knowledge of self love and explained that self love used freely was all she would need to transform her world into whatever she desired.

Human Woman began to create with this love and found that through her creations, she had given birth to herself, and through birthing herself, had transformed her world.

REJUVENATION

Soma walked wearily to the home of the healer Umina. His body sagged and was filled with pain after a long bout of infections.

"When did the first one come?" he wondered to himself, observing the vibrancy of the life all around him, so very different now from his own energy. "Oh yes, it was after the flood two years ago. Has it really been that long?"

He'd worked with several healers over these two years and was now exhausted and discouraged. Each illness had healed, only to be followed shortly by a different one and no one seemed able to find why his body was so weak that it couldn't grab onto health again. The last healer who worked with Soma had suggested he seek out Umina who was known for unusual but very effective methods in the treatment of undiagnosable illnesses.

Soma arrived at Umina's prepared to stay for three days as Umina had requested. And there stood Umina, gentle eyes observing Soma's painful approach. Within the small building, part stone and part cave, Umina had a fire burning, several blankets spread on the floor, a sleeping area, and a healing cradle that was deeply cushioned, covered with soft bedding and set upon a platform about waist high. After some time of discussing Soma's ailments, Umina directed him to remove all of his clothing and jewelry and lay himself, unburdened by life's symbols, into the healing cradle.

The healing began slowly, Umina cleared energy around them with burning sage, cedar and myrrh. He drew their heart beats into unity with earth and spirit through drum's voice and then he instructed Soma to draw the life energy out from every cell in his body, to completely remove his life force from this ailing body into the body of his soul. As Umina watched the life withdrawing from Soma's body into the body of Soma's

108

soul, he instructed the ailing man to now raise his soul body three feet above his physical body and turn over to face himself.

Soma tried this a few times before he succeeded and was able to hold his energy steady without re-entering his physical body. Soma's body was now in a deep sleep and Umina communicated directly with his soul. Umina found that Soma's soul and body had been working out of harmony with one another for several years. Communication between body and soul had become unclear and they were no longer working as one.

Umina showed Soma how to reach into his body and gently massage nerves, lymph nodes and brain cells until the blood flowed freely through and around them, washing away what was no longer useful and bringing fresh energy to each exhausted organ. He guided Soma to touch gently any areas that held pain, and how to discern the point at which illness had entered his body and heal that weak spot.

After one full day and night, Umina ceased his instruction and retired to his sleeping area, leaving Soma, body and soul, at the healing cradle. Umina slept soundly for two nights and one day, joining with spirit as an energy source for Soma's soul. And Soma continued to work on his body, touching, resting, touching, resting, as his wisdom guided him.

On the morning of the third day, Umina awoke with the sun at dawn and moved to Soma's side. During the night, Soma's soul had reseated in his body and now his cells were again glowing with the vibrancy of life energy. Umina observed Soma for a few hours, watching his aura grow stronger and more vivid. He prepared a meal of light, fresh foods and clear water to drink then sat quietly, waiting to greet Soma upon his full return to his body.

Soma's eyes opened hesitantly, he stretched his fingers and toes a bit and looked around, trying to recall where he was and how long he'd been sleeping. He noticed Umina and remembered this was a healer's place. He remembered a voice talking to him in his sleep, asking what he would do with his life when his vibrancy resumed, asking him if he chose life or death. He remembered choosing life and he remembered choosing to continue with the course he walked prior to his illness. Soma remembered singing to his body, the song rising up from every part of his soul and rushing forth to his body until his whole body vibrated with the tones of his soul, every cell echoing the song to its neighbors. He drew breath deep into his body and felt a surge of energy that had become foreign in the last few years, and he knew his body and soul once again danced in harmony.

Soma gratefully shared the meal Umina offered him and at sunset of the third day, he left Umina's healing place and joyfully returned to life.

DREAM

We walk today through the cities, villages, and countrysides that once were ruled by oppressive customs. On our right is Africa, regal, jungled, proud Africa. Where once we saw deserts, starvation, dead stumps of the ancient jungles, today we see strong, healthy women, men, and children. Their beauty glowing in the sunlight and moonlight as they move about their lives.

On our left is South America, land of the great American rain forest, the mighty Amazon River and the jagged Andes Mountains. When last we walked through this place her people were crowding deeper and deeper into the jungle, her skies dark with smoke as the jungle burned in advance of the people. Today, children smile brightly at us and sing as they wind their ways among the trees, following the trails of four legged friends to the cool banks of a river. Beyond South America we see the Pacific Islands, glowing, green jewels in a sea of deep green water.

Come now, walk further north and we see Central America, blooming and beautiful, her people well fed and at peace. We see the Middle East, sand sparkling like diamonds in the sunlight. Her olive trees and cypress, those ancient symbols of peaceful times, cover the hillsides, undisturbed for generations.

And further over, looking into the morning sun, we see the colorful lands of Asia. National borders have long since disappeared and the peaceful ways of those ancient cultures once again thrive.

Come further north yet, to Europe and North America, the lands where snow falls and the forests grow slowly. Do you remember when these lands had more people than trees? Do you remember when the people lived crowded on top of each other, stacking apartments three or four, or in some places, dozens, high so there would be enough room? When there was seldom a time or a place that lacked human noise? Look now, the people are quieter, outnumbered by the trees. They live in homes that touch Earth, they walk daily on Earth. They sleep only a few feet from her surface, not perched in the sky like winged ones.

Pause here with me, standing still in the midst of the great Atlantic Ocean. Look far to the north and see that all is well for the icy cloak of the Arctic flashes her greeting to us. Look far to the south where the ice of the Antarctic flashes a response. Look, the craters left by mining and the bombs of so many wars have worn into peaceful hollows filled with green growing ones. Everywhere we look the tree people stand tall and strong, whispering as the winds of Earth comb their mighty branches. The water at our feet runs clear and full of swimming ones. Their brilliant colors flash daily near the shores. The winged people and the four leggeds move easily among the two leggeds. They share paths, food, and shelter. Look now at the two leggeds. We have learned. We have learned to be in good relationship with all of Earth's dwellers. Our homes are warm and comfortable, full of food, love, and laughter. Our faces, in every place we dwell, are lit with smiles. Our voices carry tones of tenderness. We move gently and with confidence, knowing we too are the magikal and well loved children of Earth.

Remember, our world was once a dream too. All dreams are dreams until someone begins to live them.

ABOUT THE AUTHOR

Laughing Womyn Ashonosheni is a priestess, healer, visionary, and a spiritual teacher. In her many years of facilitating spiritual growth through working with individuals in private sessions, leadership in ritual circles, and teaching classes and seminars she has consistently encouraged wholeness through open hearts and self-responsibility. Her vision is to help create a world in which each person is so filled with delight that the concepts of violence and abuse dissolve from our realm of possibilities.

INDEX OF GODDESSES AND GODS

Amaterasu – sun goddess, Japan
Am-mit – underworld goddess, Egypt
Ataksak – god of joy, Eskimo
Athtor – night goddess, Egypt
Atri – wisdom, Hindu
Awhiowhio – god of whirlwinds, Aborigine
Ayizan – mother of humans, Haiti
Baiame – moon god, Aborigine
Brigid – fertility goddess, Ireland
Calafia – Amazon queen, Amerindian
Ceres – grain goddess, Rome
Cernunnos – horned god, Celtic
Cerridwen – mother goddess, Wales
Changing Woman – Amerindian goddess
Chasca – goddess of maidens, Inca
Citallinicue – Milky Way goddess, Aztec
Coyote – trickster, Amerindian
Cuchavira – god of healing and childbirth, Colombia
Dana – mother goddess, Ireland
Dionysus – wine and fertility god, Greece
Eir – healer, Teutonic
Faunus – nature god, Rome
Feng P'O-P'O – wind goddess, China
Frey – fertility god, Scandinavia
Fu-Hsing – god of happiness, China
Gaia – earth goddess, Greece
Gendenwitha – morning star, Iroquois
Ghede – death god, Haiti

Gokarmo – mother goddess, Tibet
Hagia Sophia – wisdom goddess, Greece
Hakea – goddess of dead, Hawaii
Hekate – underworld goddess, Greece
Hina – first woman, Maori
Hotei – god of laughter, Japan
Hsi-Ho – mother of the suns, China
Igaehindvo – sun goddess, Cherokee
Kama – love god, Hindu
Karu – creator of mountains, Brazil
Kefa – mother of time, Egypt
Knowee – sun goddess, Aborigine
Kozah – storm god, Persia
Kuan-Ti – war god, China
Kupala – god of joy, Slavonic
Lucina – goddess of light, Eastern Europe
Meztli – night goddess, Aztec
Nahar – sun goddess, Syria
Nammu – ocean goddess, Sumerian
Nataraja – god of dance, Hindu
Ninkarrak – healer, Chaldean
Notus – god of the south wind, Greece
Nox – night goddess, Rome
Nyx – night goddess, Greece
Omacatl – god of happiness, Aztec
Potos – god of desire, Phoenician
Prisni – earth goddess, Hindu
Prometheus – wise advice, Greece
Purutabbui – creator of stars, Pericu
Qat – creator god, Australia
Rait – sun goddess, Egypt
Raka – full moon goddess, Hindu

Ran – ocean goddess, Teutonic
Ratri – night goddess, Hindu
Sarasvati – goddess of the arts, Hindu
Sedna – goddess of animals, Eskimo
Shai – god of destiny, Egypt
Shapash – sun goddess, Sumerian
Skadi – huntress, Teutonic
Soma – moon god, Hindu
Spider Woman—Amerindian
Sul – sun goddess, British
Surya – sun goddess, Hindu
Tannus – thunder god, Gaelic
Tecciztecatl – moon goddess, Aztec
Telepinu – fertility god, Hittite
Umina – god of medicine, Ecuador
Vasanti – woodland goddess, Hindu
Wurusemu – sun goddess, Hittite
Yama – first man, Hindu
Yetl – thunder raven, Athapascan
Yhi – sun goddess, Aborigine
Zamba – creator god, Yaunde
Zorya Vechernyaya – sunset goddess, Slavonic

5799874R00079

Printed in Great Britain
by Amazon.co.uk, Ltd.,
Marston Gate.